A LOVING CURE

"How does your side feel?" Betty asked
Fargo.

"I think I'm going to live," he said, closing
his arms around her. Lifting her chin, he
kissed her full on the lips. He had expected
a chaste response, but what he got instead
was an embrace so fiery he felt his head
spin.

"I was beginning to wonder if you were *ever*
going to do that," she said with a sigh of
pleasure.

"It's not been easy keeping myself from it and
that's a fact," Fargo chuckled.

"Why on earth should you keep yourself
from doing it?" she demanded. "It's all I've
wanted since you came here," she said as
she reached out and began unbuckling his
belt. . . .

SHARPS JUSTICE

by
Jon Sharpe

A SIGNET BOOK

NEW AMERICAN LIBRARY

PUBLISHED BY
THE NEW AMERICAN LIBRARY
OF CANADA LIMITED

NAL BOOKS ARE AVAILABLE AT QUANTITY DISCOUNTS WHEN USED
TO PROMOTE PRODUCTS OR SERVICES. FOR INFORMATION PLEASE WRITE TO
PREMIUM MARKETING DIVISION, NEW AMERICAN LIBRARY, 1633 BROADWAY,
NEW YORK, NEW YORK 10019.

The first chapter in this book previously appeared in *Red River
Revenge*, the thirty-third volume in this series.

First Signet Printing, October, 1984

2   3   4   5   6   7   8   9

 SIGNET TRADEMARK REG. U.S. PAT. OFF. AND FOREIGN COUNTRIES
REGISTERED TRADEMARK — MARCA REGISTRADA
HECHO EN WINNIPEG, CANADA

SIGNET, SIGNET CLASSIC, MENTOR, PLUME, MERIDIAN
and NAL BOOKS are published in Canada by The New American
Library of Canada, Limited, Scarborough, Ontario.

PRINTED IN CANADA
COVER PRINTED IN U.S.A.

The Trailsman

Beginnings ... they bend the tree and they mark the man. Skye Fargo was born when he was eighteen. Terror was his midwife, vengeance his first cry. Killing spawned Skye Fargo, ruthless, cold-blooded murder. Out of the acrid smoke of gunpowder still hanging in the air, he rose, cried out a promise never forgotten.

The Trailsman, they began to call him, all across the West: searcher, scout, hunter, the man who could see where others only looked, his skills for hire but not his soul, the man who lived each day to the fullest, yet trailed each tomorrow. Skye Fargo, the Trailsman, the seeker who could take the wildness of a land and the wanting of a woman and make them his own.

1861—high in the Bitterroots, where the crack of a Sharps and the powerful jaws of a grizzly bring final justice . . .

1

Dismounting from his pinto, Skye Fargo stretched luxuriously. Then he led his mount down through the cool pines to the bank of the swift mountain stream, the music of which had drawn him from the ridge above.

This had been an unusually dry summer and autumn. Though winter would soon be clothing this high country in deep white drifts, since sunup Fargo had been traversing a seared upland plateau where the few waterholes he could find had already dried up. That afternoon he had passed an abandoned road ranch, its well as dry as a gopher hole, the few remaining stock running wild and gaunt.

Fargo was careful not to let the pinto drink too deeply, too quickly, and only after the pony's thirst had been quenched did he pluck his hat off and duck his head under the swift flow, reveling in the stream's icy shock. Lifting his head from the water, he ran a powerful hand through his thick black hair. Then he bent once more to the stream, cupping the water in his hands. Sloppily, greedily, he drank, delighting in the chill that came from the icy rivulets that streamed down his chest.

His thirst slaked, Fargo filled his hat with water and approached the pinto. The handsome Ovaro nodded in eagerness as Fargo lifted the streaming hat to his snout. As soon as the pony had drunk its fill, Fargo clapped his hat back on, letting what water remained in it cascade down over his face and neck.

For a moment he stood beside the pinto, his keen lake-blue eyes glancing alertly about him. A powerfully built man better than six feet tall, he had a waist almost as narrow as a woman's. Ridging his soaked deerskin shirt were heavy, cabled muscles that stood out like mole tunnels. His neck resembled a young tree trunk and was rooted in shoulders so broad he must have had to move sideways to enter most cabin doorways. But it was Skye Fargo's face that no man—or woman—ever forgot. Wide across the brow and cheekbones, his face was dominated by a rock-solid chin and a powerful blade of a nose. It was this last that imparted to him his fierce, eaglelike watchfulness.

At the moment Fargo's destination was Deer Lodge, a small hamlet hidden deep in the Bitterroots, a jumping-off point for settlers on their way to Oregon—a town rumored to be an ideal hideout for road agents and rustlers on the run. There was a chance the two men he sought might have chosen to hole up there. It was only a chance, but as always, it was this that drove Fargo on—and that would continue to do so until he found those he sought.

The cool, bracing scent of the pines relaxed him. He hunkered down, then leaned his back against a pine. He had expected to ride into Deer Lodge a little after sundown, but was now considering the advantages of camping where he was for the night. The soiled towns of men always left a stench in his nostrils, one he found difficult to eradicate. But this stream beside which he now sat filled the woodland with a music and his soul with a contentment that was already lulling him.

The distant crack of a rifle broke the stillness.

Fargo was on his feet instantly. The detonation had come from the other side of the ridge he had just left. Again the rifle spoke. Alert on the instant, Fargo snaked his Sharps from his pony's scabbard and started back up through the pines with the speed and silence of a great cat.

As he reached the ridge, the rifle sounded again— from somewhere in the rocks below him. Fargo heard the heavy *thwack* of a slug slamming into its target. He kept going on down the slope until he glimpsed through the pines what appeared to be a settler's wagon. It was at a standstill. Again the rifle cracked below him. This time Fargo saw a tendril of smoke curling up from a pile of rocks off to his right.

Fargo kept angling down the slope. Soon he was close enough to see most of the wagon through the pines. A steady stream of water was gushing from a hole in one of the water barrels strapped to its side and an oxen was lying on its side in the traces. Since there had been no answering fire from the wagon,

Fargo could only conclude that the settler had no weapons with a range capable of reaching the sniper.

Moving much more cautiously now, Fargo crept across the slope until the man firing on the wagon became visible. He lay behind an embedded, cinderlike stone of volcanic origin. As Fargo watched, the sniper lifted his rifle to his shoulder, aimed carefully, and fired again. A pine branch above the second oxen's head separated as the round sliced through it. At this stage then, he was simply trying to terrorize the settlers in the wagon.

Fargo studied the ground between himself and the sniper, noting several ravines and a stand of piñon that clung to a gravel slope. If he kept himself between the splash of timber and the sniper, he could cat-foot it down there without showing himself to the sniper. He picked his way on down the slope, cut straight through the piñon, and came out behind a granite upthrust. Positioning himself carefully, he lifted the Sharps and drew a bead on the sniper, whose attention was riveted on the wagon.

"Drop that rifle," Fargo called down to him, his powerful voice reaching effortlessly down the slope.

The sniper froze. Without turning his head, he said, "Who's that?"

"Never mind who it is."

The man hesitated. Fargo chuckled and tucked the stock more securely into his shoulder. "That's right," he said. "Give me an excuse."

"Not so fast, stranger," the sniper said, still facing the wagon. "I'll be glad to cut you in."

"I'm already in. And this here rifle is trained on your back. So don't make no sudden moves."

Carefully, the sniper set his rifle down on a rock beside him and rolled over to a sitting position. As he did so, his floppy-brimmed, black hat fell off. He was wearing a sheepskin coat over a red flannel shirt, which was unbuttoned, revealing a chest covered with a mass of coiled, rust-colored hair. He was a man in his mid-thirties with a broad, powerful barrel of a figure. A red stubble covered his face, a matching counterpart to the full head of flaming red hair that topped his powerful bullet-shaped head. The only thing clean about him was the gleaming Colt sitting in his tied-down, oiled holster—that, and the Bull Durham tag dangling from his coat pocket.

"Get up," Fargo said, picking his way down the slope to the fellow. "And keep your hands away from your body where I can see them."

"Damn you all to hell! How'd you get so close?" The man's eyes held a mad light in them as he peered furiously at Fargo. "What are you anyway, some goddamn breed?"

Fargo's Indian blood was apparent, he knew, in his raven-black hair, but he felt no need to answer this man. "Use your left hand to unbuckle your gun belt," Fargo told him.

As the fellow unbuckled his gun belt and let it fall to the slope, he glared at Fargo, his face hard. "You still got a chance to cut yourself in," he said. "With no hard feelin's. You can have half of what's in that wagon."

"Move on down the slope."

"Damn your hide! Listen to me."

"Turn around," Fargo told him. "I'm losing my patience." Fargo's voice was dangerously low.

13

Slowly, grudgingly, the man turned about and started down the slope. Fargo picked up the man's gunbelt and rifle, moved closer to him, and placed the barrel of his Sharps in the small of his back. Then he pushed, hard. The big man lurched forward and went toppling headlong down the slope. Fargo followed as swiftly as he could after him. When the sniper's tumbling body came to rest finally, he was almost beside the wagon.

Pulling up beside him, Fargo glanced over and saw a bonneted woman peering out at him from behind the wagon. Her face was white with terror, her eyes wide. She was clutching a pitchfork in her hands.

"You all right, ma'am?" Fargo inquired.

She took a step back, then blurted, "My husband. He's shot!"

Fargo stepped closer to her and glanced down the length of the wagon. A wounded man was sitting up, his back to the front wheel, an ancient flintlock pistol in his hand. Fargo was impressed. It was with this feeble weapon that the settler had been able to keep the big redhead at bay.

"You hurt bad?" Fargo asked him.

"I'll make it," the settler replied gamely.

Fargo returned to the sniper as the man struggled to his feet. His tumble down the slope had torn his shirt and ripped a long gash in his sheepskin. There was a wide scratch running down one side of his face. As he stood there, feet wide, glowering malevolently at Fargo, he looked just crazy enough to charge.

"Walk over to the rear of the wagon," Fargo told him.

The sniper hesitated a moment, as if he were deliberating whether or not to do what Fargo told him. Fargo smiled slightly and released the safety on his Sharps.

"Go ahead, you son of a bitch," Fargo said softly. "Make it easy for me."

The big redhead looked away from Fargo, then walked past him to the rear of the wagon. As he came to a halt behind the wagon, Fargo threw the man's weapons into it, then he stepped closer and cracked the redhead on the side of his skull with the barrel of his Sharps. It was a mean crack, and the big fellow's knees sagged. He groped out blindly for the tailgate. For a moment, it looked as if it would take another blow from Fargo's Sharps to render him completely unconscious, but then he sagged slowly to the ground. Bending down, Fargo flung the man over his shoulder, straightened, turned, and flung him like an oversized sack of potatoes into the rear of the wagon.

Then he walked past the woman to the other side of the wagon and looked down at her wounded husband.

"How bad you hit?" he asked the man.

"Nothing vital," the fellow replied, trying to grin. "Ericson caught me in the shoulder."

"That his name?"

The settler nodded. "Red Ericson. He just got run out of Deer Lodge."

"We're the Johnsons," the woman said. "I'm Mary Jane and this here's my husband, Tom."

Fargo told them his name. Then he knelt beside the settler, pulled back his shirt, and saw the angry red hole punched in the skin where the slug had entered. The entry wound was low enough for the slug to have shattered the man's shoulder bone. Most of the bleeding was coming from the back of the shoulder, where the bullet had exited.

Fargo stood up. "How far are we from Deer Lodge?"

"An hour," Tom said. "Maybe two."

"All right then. I'll ride back there with you. Think you can make it to Deer Lodge with only one ox?"

Mary Jane spoke up then. "Yes," she said, nodding determinedly as she brushed a lock of hair off her forehead. "I'm sure we can."

Fargo smiled. He believed her.

Fargo rode into Deer Lodge a few minutes before sundown, the wagon trailing some distance behind, the settler's wife up on the seat. The town's evident prosperity surprised Fargo. Considering its reputation, he had not expected anything remotely resembling what he saw.

Well-constructed frame buildings lined both sides of the main street, and some of them were painted. Across from the hotel there was a large stable, and alongside it a large general store in back of which Fargo glimpsed a tangle of sheds and stables along with piles of fresh lumber. Next to the general store was a barbershop, a blacksmith shop, and two saloons. Across the street another saloon, the largest one in town. It was attached to the hotel, an imposing three-story frame building, painted white with green trim. Alongside the hotel stood a newly constructed jailhouse, the wood still raw and unpainted. Beside it was a restaurant, then a second general store. At the far end of the street, a feed mill sat beside the plank bridge spanning the creek.

Deer Lodge looked like a town that had settled in to stay.

As Fargo reined up in front of the hotel, two men left the saloon to look him over. Then one of the men pointed to the wagon trailing Fargo and shouted to the others still inside. Immediately, a small gang of men crowded out through the batwings.

"Is there a lawman here?" Fargo asked, dismounting and dropping his reins over the hitch rack.

A lean, long-faced individual pushed through the crowd on the porch. "That'd be me," he told Fargo. "Name's Sheriff Wills. Who're you, stranger?"

"Name's Fargo. Skye Fargo."

"What's up?"

"I just brought Tom Johnson and his wife back. Red Ericson tried to bushwhack them. Looks like he was after their wagon and goods."

Wills frowned quickly, his face filled with sudden concern. "Ericson, you say?"

"That's the one."

"And he shot up the Johnsons?"

Fargo nodded. "Tom was the only one hit."

"How bad is he?" someone in the crowd wanted to know.

"He'll need someone to look after his shoulder," Fargo replied. "He's in the back of the wagon with Ericson."

"I'll get Doc Swenson," someone at the rear of the

17

crowd called, his booted feet hurrying off down the sidewalk.

By that time the wagon had reached the hotel and Mary Jane was pulling her single ox to a halt. At once the crowd pressed close around the wagon. Hands reached up to help Mary Jane down as other men scrambled around to the rear of the wagon and lowered the tailgate.

Fargo and Sheriff Wills walked around to the rear of the wagon to oversee things. Mary Jane and two husky men helped the wounded settler down from the wagon. He was wan and groggy, but able to move under his own power. Peering into the wagon beside Wills, Fargo saw that Ericson was still sprawled where he had dumped him, his ankles and wrists bound securely. Choosing three brawny individuals, Wills directed them to carry Ericson off to the jailhouse down the street.

As Fargo watched them go, he turned to the sheriff. "You fellows figuring on giving Ericson a trial before you hang him?"

"Why?"

"I'd be willing to testify."

Wills smiled, his eyes regarding Fargo with amusement as well as respect. "Sure. You can testify. But you'll have to stand in line with all the others. Meanwhile, I'd like to buy you a drink, Mr. Fargo."

"Suits me fine," Fargo replied, turning about and entering the saloon with the sheriff.

Fargo was led over to a table in the far corner, where a very pretty young lady was waiting. She smiled up at Wills as he approached, then glanced questioningly at Fargo.

"Cindy," Wills said to her, "this here gent is Skye Fargo. Guess who he just brought in."

"I heard," Cindy said, smiling up at Fargo. "The man-mountain himself, Red Ericson."

Fargo pulled a chair over and sat down at the table across from her. The girl was nursing a harmless ginger drink and her pert, fresh beauty looked out of place in the saloon. She had mischievous dark eyes and a heavy swirl of chestnut curls pinned carelessly onto her head. Her neck was long and graceful, her features pleasing, with a faint sprinkling of freckles across the bridge of her nose.

As Wills sat down beside the girl, he smiled proudly. "Cindy runs the new restaurant in town. And pretty soon she'll be runnin' me, too. We're getting married."

"Congratulations," Fargo said, smiling at them. "And it looks like you got something else new in town . . . beside the restaurant."

"You mean the jail."

Fargo nodded.

Willis nodded emphatically, "Part of our cleanup. This town's had its bellyful of hard cases."

"You drove them out?"

"Them as we could catch."

"Red Ericson was the worst one," said Cindy, shuddering slightly. "Last year he killed a man."

Wills explained. "The stupid oaf was in his cups. A local hardware clerk no bigger than a toothpick questioned Red about something, and Red picked him up, carried him outside, and dunked him head down into a full rain barrel. By the time he pulled him out again, the clerk had drowned."

"And you didn't string Ericson up for that?"

"Ericson and the rest of his buddies insisted it was just a joke," Wills explained bitterly, "that Ericson hadn't meant to kill him."

Cindy reached over and rested her hand on Wills' arm. "Deer Lodge didn't have a sheriff then," she said.

The barkeep came over with a bottle of whiskey and two glasses. When Fargo tried to pay him, the man waved Fargo off. "Your money's no good around here, mister," the barkeep said, heading back toward the bar.

Wills smiled at Fargo. "He's thanking you for bringing in Ericson. When we ran the other hard cases out of here, Ericson gave us a lot of trouble. The town council warned him if he came back, we'd make him wish he hadn't."

"Those others you sent packing—I'd like a description of them."

Wills looked at him closely. "Why? You wouldn't be a bounty hunter, would you?"

"Not exactly."

Wills filled Fargo's glass and his own, then proceeded to give Fargo as complete a description as he could of the gang of outcasts and gunslingers who, until a few months ago, had just about taken over Deer Lodge. When he finished his melancholy catalog, he leaned back in his chair and peered carefully at Fargo.

"Anyone in that gang the one you're after?" he asked.

Fargo felt tired suddenly. He shook his head. "I'm after two men, Wills. But neither one was in that bunch."

"Sorry to hear that," Wills said, his tone genuinely sympathetic.

Fargo took the whiskey bottle and poured himself another drink. Then, to change the subject, he turned with a smile to Cindy and asked her if she had been able yet to get the sheriff to agree to a wedding date. She had, she replied laughing, and then both of them invited Fargo to stay for it. Fargo could tell that they genuinely and sincerely wanted him to become a part of their wedding.

He was almost tempted to do so.

Still lying facedown on the bunk where he had been roughly deposited, Ericson—now fully conscious—waited.

The rawhide Fargo had used to bind the redhead's hands and feet had been cut loose, and though he was famished, Ericson had not touched the tray of food that had been left for him on the small table inside the cell. Jails and lawmen were new to this town, and Ericson had almost laughed aloud when he regained consciousness and saw where Wills' deputy had left the food tray.

The door to the cell block opened. Abe Zuckerman entered and peered at him. Groaning softly, Ericson pulled his body into a ball and cowered with his back to the wall.

"My head," he cried hoarsely, "my head. I been hurt bad, Abe. I can barely see."

Zuckerman pulled up and peered through the

bars, evidently feeling some satisfaction at Ericson's condition.

"Well, now," he drawled, shifting his chaw to the other cheek. "Ain't that too bad."

"Please," Ericson gasped painfully, squinting through the bars at Zuckerman. "You got to get the doc."

"I don't got to do nothing," Abe replied, chuckling.

"Yes, you do," Ericson whined.

Zuckerman spat a glob of tobacco juice on the new floor and peered past Ericson's cowering body at the still-untouched tray of food. The man quickly moistened his lips.

"Ain't you even touched your food," Zuckerman asked hopefully.

"I can't eat, Abe," Ericson told him. "Not in my condition."

Zuckerman selected a key and opened the cell door. With only a cursory glance at Ericson, he strode into the cell and reached for the tray of food. Before his hand had closed about it, Ericson struck.

Uncoiling from the cot like a giant snake, he flung himself upon Abe, his two hands closing about the deputy's scrawny neck. Lifting him up off the floor, Ericson shook him as a cat would a mouse, then flung him against the wall, headfirst. As Abe thrashed feebly, Ericson reached for the long skinning knife sheathed in the small of his back, bent swiftly, and slit Zuckerman's throat.

Doing what he could to avoid the sudden freshet of blood, Ericson lifted the deputy's six-gun from his holster and darted from the cell. Moving with surprising lightness for a man his size, he reached the still-open door the deputy had come through and nudged it gently wider, then peered carefully into the outer office.

It was empty.

Ericson straightened, disappointed. He had hoped to find Wills at his desk. He hated Wills and would have liked nothing better than to have disposed of him as he had Zimmerman.

Stepping into the room, Ericson walked over to the window and peered out. Diagonally across from the jailhouse was the hotel's saloon. It was nearly twilight and there were not many people on the street. Racked alongside the settler's wagon in front of the hotel were two powerful saddle horses. One was a chestnut, the other a big black. Ericson smiled. That black would do nicely. He strode over to the wall rack and lifted his gun belt down off the wooden peg. Strapping it on, he loaded the Colt and tied the holster's thongs around his thigh. Then he reached up and took down his rifle. He found cartridges in the sheriff's desk, loaded the rifle, then dropped the box of cartridges into his jacket pocket.

Opening the jailhouse door, he stepped out and strode boldly across the street toward the saloon. No one glanced in his direction or took any notice of him as he dropped his rifle into the big black's scabbard, then untied the horse from the hitch rack. He was about to mount the horse when he glanced up at the hotel's saloon. Sheriff Wills liked to frequent this place, Ericson knew, and was probably in there right now. And maybe that big son of a bitch who had dealt himself in was with him.

Ericson's stubbled face went hard with resolve.

Resting his right hand lightly on his Colt's grips, he stepped up onto the saloon porch and strode toward the batwings. Before he reached them, a patron left the saloon, clapping his hat on as he stepped out onto the porch. When he saw Ericson, he stopped in midstride and appeared ready to cry out.

Before he could utter a sound, Ericson clubbed the man viciously on the side of the head with the barrel of his Colt. The man slumped to the floor of the porch. Ericson stepped over the sprawled body and shouldered his way through the batwings.

2

Fargo saw the look on Wills' face and turned.

What he saw in that instant was Red Ericson standing in the saloon doorway, a big six-gun in his hand, the batwings still flipping behind him. Cindy, on her way out of the saloon, had halted in her tracks. The four men at the bar were staring in shock at Ericson. The bartender—in the act of polishing a glass—stood paralyzed, his mouth open, his eyes wide. On the other side of the door two poker players at a table along the wall were looking up from their game. The one Fargo knew as Tim had already seen Ericson.

"Jesus," said Wills softly.

Fargo heard the sheriff's chair scraping along the floor as he sprang to his feet. Fargo went for his Colt. Ericson aimed at Fargo. But a second before the big Colt detonated, Fargo felt Wills hit him from behind, knocking him out of his chair. Fargo hit the floor on his hands and knees, then continued to sprawl forward as the full weight of the sheriff's body bore him to the floor, partially immobilizing him.

One of the men at the bar drew his six-gun as did the poker player Tim. With the speed of a striking rattlesnake, Ericson snatched Cindy and drew her in front of him, using her body as a shield. Holstering his six-gun, he drew a long buffalo-skinning knife and held it against Cindy's neck. Then he took a step backward, pulling the girl along with him.

"Don't any of you move," he snarled, "or I'll slice this pretty throat."

"You won't get away with this, Red," the poker player cried, his face dark with fury.

Ignoring him, Ericson pressed the blade closer against Cindy's throat. A thin tracery of blood sprang from her neck. "If I see a posse—or if I see any of you coming after me," Ericson cried, "I'll kill her and take my chances. You let me ride out of here without no trouble—and you give me a week, I'll let her go."

"You expect us to believe that?" the barkeep asked.

"What choice you got?" Ericson snarled, grinning.

Then he drew his six-gun and threw a shot at Fargo, who was still sprawled on the floor. Then he vanished out the door, dragging Cindy after him. Fargo flung himself to his feet and drew his gun to go after him. But the bartender and Tim stepped between him and the door.

"No," the bartender cried. "Let the son of a bitch go! He'll kill Cindy if we don't."

"She's dead already," Fargo said.

"Mebbe so," said Tim, "but we got to give her a chance. We just got to!"

Fargo could find no reason to argue with that. He relaxed and holstered his six-gun. A moment later they heard two horses galloping off down the street. Tim and his poker-playing partner rushed out onto the porch and returned a moment later, their faces cold with fury. Red Ericson had taken their horses: a chestnut and a powerful black stallion.

The tension in the saloon relaxed somewhat, and for the first time Fargo realized he had been hit in the forearm. Glancing down, he saw it was just a flesh wound, more like a burn than a puncture wound. It was hardly bleeding.

"Hey!" someone cried. "What's the matter with Wills?"

Fargo spun about. The sheriff was still sprawled on the floor, a dark pool of blood seeping steadily out from under him. Fargo hurried back and knelt beside Wills as the saloon's patrons crowded around.

Wills turned his head and looked up at Fargo. His face was as gray as an old newspaper.

"Where's Cindy, Fargo?"

"Ericson took her."

"You've got to go after him."

"We'll both go."

"No," Wills said feebly, shaking his head. "Not me. I'm hurt bad."

"Where?"

"In the side."

Fargo found the wound. The sheriff was right. The bullet had ranged up under his rib cage, tearing up his lungs fearfully. In addition to the blood pulsing

27

from his side, a thin trace was trickling from his mouth.

"Dammit, Wills," Fargo said softly, bitterly. "You should have jumped the other way. That slug you took was meant for me."

"Never mind that," Wills rasped, his voice barely audible. "Go after Cindy for me. Bring her back. Get her out of that killer's hands."

"I will. That's a promise."

Wills appeared satisfied. He let his head sag to the floor. Fargo stood up, looked down at him for a moment, then turned away as the doctor hurried anxiously into the saloon.

As the doctor brushed past him, Fargo did not bother to tell him he was too late.

The townspeople buried Frank Wills and Abe Zuckerman the next day on a knoll above town, some distance from the other boot hill they had used to bury the hard cases and outlaws who had bought their own blazing deaths before Deer Lodge, with the aid of men like Frank Wills, had cleansed itself.

The breath of winter was in the air. In the cold sunlight Fargo stood apart, watching. When at last both coffins were lowered into their separate graves, he turned and walked alone back down the hill to the hotel saloon. Except for the barkeep, the place was empty. Fargo walked up to the bar and ordered a bottle of bourbon. He sampled it, then stoppered it. He intended to include it among his provisions.

As he paid for the bourbon, the barkeep said, "Mind if I ask you a question?"

Fargo shook his head.

"You going after Cindy Talcott?"

"Yes."

"You heard what Red said he'd do if he saw anyone tailin' him before a week was out. He means it. I wouldn't put anything past that bastard."

"Neither would I, but I promised Wills I'd go after her."

"Maybe you better wait a week. Red might let her go, like he said he would."

"Do you really believe that?"

The barkeep's eyes dropped to the top of the bar. A frown on his face, he polished a spot with his towel. Then he glanced up at Fargo and shook his head. "Guess maybe I don't, at that."

"Besides," Fargo went on, "if I wait a full week, Ericson will be long gone. We've already given him all night and most of this morning. That should be enough to lull him. I'll stay out of sight. Don't worry."

Tim entered the saloon. When he saw Fargo, he came over. "I thought I'd find you here," he said. "Word is you're goin' after Ericson today. You ain't waitin'."

"You heard right."

He nodded, satisfied. "Then maybe you ought to hear what Biff Moffet's got to tell you. He's waitin' outside."

"What's this all about, Tim?"

"Moffet saw Cindy and Ericson."

Fargo snatched his bottle off the bar and left the saloon with Tim.

The settler Biff Moffet was a long, sinewy drink of water in bib overalls and a large, floppy-brimmed, black hat. His long hair hung in lank coils down onto his shoulder, and his shave had been a careless, indifferent job, accomplished, Fargo had no doubt, in cold water. The man was waiting for them beside his wagon in front of the general store.

"This here's Biff Moffet, Fargo," Tim said.

Fargo shook the sodbuster's rough hand.

"You the one goin' after Ericson?" Moffet asked.

Fargo nodded. "What can you tell me?"

"I was in my barn along about sundown yesterday," the settler said, "when Ericson rode up. He was leadin' a woman. When they got close enough, I could see her feet was lashed together under her horse and her hands was tied to the saddle horn. I know Red can be bad trouble, so I ran to my cabin and got my rifle. I was just in time to drive him off." He paused, waiting for their expressions of approval.

"Dammit, Moffet," Tim said. "Go on."

Moffet cleared his throat. "What I did was I fired a couple of shots over his head. He pulled up and threatened to kill the girl he was with if I didn't let him take one of my horses. I told him to take one from the barn and ride out." Biff Moffet shook his head unhappily. "Red has a good eye, damn the son of a bitch. He took my best pack horse."

"Which way did he go?"

"Northwest, toward the pass. You think I'll ever see that horse of mine again?"

"Hell, man," Tim exploded. "What do *you* think?"

"Just wonderin'," the settler replied unhappily. "And maybe hopin'. My wife, she don't think so neither."

"The girl," Fargo said, stepping closer, "how was she taking it?"

Moffet frowned. "Not so good," he replied. "No, sir. She acted mighty strange. She looked all cried out. Know what I mean? She didn't say a word. Even when I fired over Ericson's head. It was kinda scary, the way she sat her horse, staring straight ahead, her face without no expression."

Fargo didn't like the sound of that. He said nothing further to the settler and thanked him.

As Moffet turned and entered the general store, Tim turned to Fargo, his face drawn with concern. "You better let me go with you," he said.

"No sense in that, Tim. Thanks just the same. I'm just moving on through this here valley anyway. Two men on Ericson's tail would lift too much dust. He's liable to catch on we're tailin' him and do as he threatened."

Tim considered the sense of this, then nodded reluctantly.

They walked back to the hotel, where Fargo's already saddled pinto was waiting at the hitch rack. Fargo tucked the bottle of bourbon into his saddlebag, then mounted up. Leaning over, he shook Tim's hand. A small crowd of grim, silent townsmen gathered as he pulled the pinto back from the rail and started down the street. Not a man called out any encouragement, and none of them smiled. They knew on what a grim, futile mission he was embarking. Only a few waved.

Fargo waved back, and a moment later his horse clattered across the wooden bridge as he headed northwest, toward the pass.

*   *   *

It was near the end of a long four-day ride when Fargo approached a settler's place high in the Bitterroots. The cabin and barn were perched on the edge of a stream-fed meadowland. The soil at this altitude was thin, the grass precariously rooted. Up this high the growing season had to be short, the winters brutal.

The cabin was ringed with piñon stumps. Its roof was of sod squares and its ridgepole sagged. The privy sat crookedly behind the cabin on an uneven hole dug halfheartedly from the stony soil. The front yard was littered with a remarkable collection of junk: a rusted hay mower, a rotting mattress, the broken, weed-infested bed of a farm wagon, and an overturned grindstone. Only the tall pole barn seemed the result of any solid effort on the sodbuster's part.

A flock of Rhode Island Reds feeding just outside the corral scattered, cackling in confusion at his approach. A large ragged-looking collie left the barn, watched him sullenly for a moment, then began to bark.

This brought the settler out of the cabin. He was carrying a Hawken. The man spoke sharply to the dog. It turned and slunk miserably back into the barn. The settler's woman, a swollen, lank-haired Indian squaw, appeared behind him in the cabin doorway. Though Fargo could not be certain from this distance, she appeared to be a woman of the Nez Percé tribe.

Fargo pulled up his pinto and folded his arms to wait until the settler lowered the long barrel of his

Hawken. When he did so finally, Fargo nodded pleasantly to him and then to his woman who was still lurking in the doorway.

"Howdy, ma'am."

She muttered something to her husband and promptly vanished from sight.

"I'm just riding through," Fargo told the settler.

The fellow regarded him sourly. His sunken cheeks and cadaverous frame bore mute testimony to his success in this region. But the eyes were sharp and alert. And mean.

"You're welcome to any water, stranger," he said, his voice almost wheedling. "And there's grain for yore hoss. And we got some potatoes and roots, if you've a mind to light and set with us a spell."

"Much obliged," Fargo replied.

"See to your hoss, then. I'll tell my woman to set another place at the table."

He turned and went back inside.

Fargo was not looking forward to the cabin's interior or the supper offered. But it was a poor sort of man who turned down any offer of hospitality on the trail.

He swung swiftly out of his saddle and led the Ovaro into the barn.

The stench that greeted Fargo when he entered the single-room cabin almost knocked him back out the door. The interior of the place was dim, lit as it was by only a single oil lamp hung from a sagging rafter. It took a moment for Fargo's stomach to accept the stench. It was one compounded of

33

unwashed bodies, swill, and carelessly emptied slops jars.

The settler had on a filthy cotton undershirt, Levi's held up by yellow braces, and mud-encrusted farm boots. His hair was graying and wild. The swollen bulk of his squaw was covered by a formless gray cotton work dress.

Huddled on the other side of the large black wood stove stood a tall, slim girl in her twenties. She regarded him warily, as would any other wild animal unaccustomed to the sight of a human being. Her hair was as long and black as her mother's, and she was dressed in a fringed deerskin dress, the skirt shiny with grease. Through a long tear in the skirt, Fargo glimpsed a portion of a silken thigh.

"I'm Matt Rawlinson," the settler said, shaking Fargo's hand. "This here's my wife, Mountain Flower." He winked broadly at Fargo. "I just call her Mountain now."

Fargo nodded to Mountain Flower.

"And that's my daughter over there, Mary Jane."

Fargo told them his name and then sat down at the bench that served as a table. As soon as the three joined him, the smell of their unwashed bodies smote him like a noxious cloud. Fargo had washed himself thoroughly at the pump outside, but it was obvious his three hosts were waiting for next spring to perform such ablutions.

The roots the settler had mentioned turned out to be turnips, together with potatoes simmering in a thick broth with chunks of succulent meat swimming in it. It was a meal hearty enough to warm Fargo's insides clear down to his boot heels, but he was careful not to ask what kind of meat was in the stew. During the meal the settler and his wife ate silently, intently, their heads down, like hogs at a trough. Mary Jane, however, occasionally peered across the table at him, her smoky eyes seeming to devour him.

When they finished the meal and the bench was cleared, Rawlinson reached down for a jug of moonshine he kept between his legs, and passed it across the table to Fargo. As Fargo lifted the jug to his lips, the smell reminded him of a mildewed silo. He gulped down a prodigious swallow, then passed the jug back. As he blinked the tears from his eyes, he wondered if he hadn't just swallowed a lighted kerosene lamp. But he kept his composure and ignored the tiny beads of perspiration standing out on his forehead.

Matt Rawlinson was watching him closely. Noting Fargo's reaction, he nodded briskly, pleased. "You took that right well," he commented.

Fargo accepted the remark as a compliment. But he said nothing. His tonsils were on fire.

Rawlinson lifted the jug high and swallowed twice. Then, wiping his mouth with the back of his hand, he passed the jug to his wife. Mountain Flower had been waiting impatiently. Snatching it from her husband, she lifted her head back and took two long swallows. Then, pausing only long enough to wipe off her mouth with the back of her hand, she lifted the jug back up and took two more prodigious gulps.

Only then did she hand the jug to Mary Jane.

Rawlinson grinned across the table at Fargo. "I don't let Mountain Flower near this here jug, less'n

35

we got guests. Like now. Mary Jane, too. Their Injun blood sure as hell takes over when that firewater hits their gut, I can tell you." His eyes lit merrily. "One night Mountain Flower came after me with a knife and sliced off part of my ear." He leaned forward and turned his head slightly so that Fargo could see the damage. "Next day she didn't remember a thing about it."

As Mary Jane was about to take another long swig, Rawlinson snatched the jug out of her hand. She glared unhappily at him for a moment, then looked away . . . at Fargo. Her eyes glowed like those of a wild cat. And Fargo could not help noticing that she appeared just as unaffected by the fiery moonshine as her mother.

"That's all," Rawlinson told the two women, stoppering the jug and putting it back down between his legs. "And if'n I catch either of you at this jug tonight, I'll whup you till yore tails drop off."

Mountain Flower turned her head slightly to gaze on her lord and master, then heaved herself to her feet and began clearing the dishes off the bench. Without a word, Mary Jane joined her.

Rawlinson leaned back and smiled at Fargo. "Where you headin', Mr. Fargo?"

"Depends. I'm looking for someone."

"Figured maybe you was. You got that look about you. A big, redheaded gent with a crazy woman in tow?"

Fargo did not like Rawlinson's reference to a crazy woman. "That sounds like the one. His name's Red Ericson. But what do you mean 'crazy woman'?"

"You know her?"

"Yes. Ericson took her hostage."

"And you want her back?"

"Yes. I promised a friend."

"Well, maybe you don't, after all," Rawlinson said. "That woman ain't right no more. That fellow Ericson's a mean one. Looks to me like he's fixed her. Fixed her real good."

"Do you want to explain that?"

"She was acting loco. Wild. Sometimes she'd sing. Other times she'd start to laughin'."

Mary Jane left her mother and stepped closer to Fargo. "It was the laughing that made me shiver," she told Fargo. "And the way she kept calling a man's name."

"Did you hear the name?"

"Sure," said Rawlinson. "The name was Frank."

Fargo nodded. "That was the man she was supposed to marry," Fargo told them grimly. "He's dead now. Killed by Ericson."

"So what's this got to do with you, Mr. Fargo?" Mary Jane asked.

"Frank was a friend of mine. I promised him I'd bring her back to Deer Lodge."

"Like I said," Rawlinson drawled, "maybe you better forget it. That woman ain't goin' to be no good to any man. Not after what that redhead's done to her."

"Pa's right," Mary Jane said.

"Get back with your ma," Rawlinson told her sharply.

The girl retreated, but she did not take her eyes off Fargo.

Fargo realized he could use some more of that moonshine.

"That son of a bitch you're after's a real bear, he is," said Rawlinson bitterly. "He got between me and the cabin and held a gun on Mary Jane. When he rode off, he was ridin' my best horse, and all he left in trade was a broke chestnut. I took after the bastard, trailed him northeast. But he caught my sign, doubled back, and shot my hoss out from under me. I had to walk back."

"He was two days gone," Mary Jane said.

Rawlinson nodded unhappily. "Just got back. Don't have a horse left now. The son of a bitch." Rawlinson reached down, lifted the jug to his lips, and took a healthy lick.

"Might there be a town he could be heading for?"

"Reckon so. Pine Bluff, if you can call it a town." Rawlinson nodded shrewdly. "Yeah. He might head for there. I heard the place is filling up with hard cases."

"How far is it?"

"Leave here at sunup and you'll make it by sundown in three days."

Fargo got to his feet, his head brushing lightly the coal-oil lamp. There was, thankfully, no place for him to sleep in the small cabin—not that he would have allowed himself to sleep here even if there were room. The smell of well-trampled horse manure and urine was infinitely preferable to the awful stench assaulting his nostrils at that moment.

"Guess I'll sleep out in the barn," he told the settler and his squaw.

The squaw spoke up then, for the first time. "Mary Jane. She show you to the barn."

Fargo was about to protest that he could find the place all by himself, but caught himself just in time.

"You like it over there?" Mary Jane said, pointing to a corner of the barn piled high with what appeared to be freshly cut hay.

"Sure," Fargo replied. "That'll be fine. Thank you."

He started for the stall where he had put the pinto, intending to get his bedroll. Mary Jane accompanied him. He began to notice that out here in the fresh air she did not smell all that bad. Perhaps if she took off that torn, grease-stained deerskin dress, she might even smell pretty good.

He dropped his bedroll onto the hay and opened the soogan. As he did so, Mary Jane went down on her knees beside him, ostensibly to help him. Their hands brushed as they both reached for the soogan's flap.

Her hand was on fire. He looked into her eyes. They were smoldering. But he could not forget how dirty her two parents were, how their stench clouded the cabin.

He stood up. She stood up also and faced him, waiting.

"I'm tired," he told her. "Exhausted. I will sure be glad to get to sleep. Thank you, Mary Jane."

"You do not want me to sleep with you tonight?"

He did not want to anger the girl. If there was one thing he had learned over the years: a good deal worse than taking a woman against her will, was *not* taking her when that was what she wanted.

He cleared his throat. "That would be nice, but

some other time," he explained carefully. "I am so tired, I do not think I could ... manage it." He shrugged and smiled.

At once she brightened.

"Get down," she said, unbuttoning her deerskin blouse. "I know how to fix that." She smiled then, her white teeth gleaming in her dark face.

When she stepped out of her skirt and stood naked before him in the dim moonlight filtering in through the barn's weathered boards, he decided not to fight it, and undressed.

As soon as he was comfortable on his soogan, she bent to him, her fiery hands cupping his flaccid penis tenderly. She stroked it for a moment. Then, with one hand, she reached under his testicles, the flame in her fingers kindling a fire that reached deep into his crotch.

Leaning over, she blew her hot breath onto the tip of his penis. Despite his reluctance, Fargo felt himself stirring to life. Mary Jane uttered a tiny, delighted squeal, then closed her hot lips about his shaft. He groaned and would have returned the favor. But he was still not sure enough of her hygiene and contented himself with running his fingers up and down her supple back. She indicated her pleasure at this, and he found her musky pubic patch gyrating inches from his head. She wriggled closer, hopefully—but he could not get himself to pull her down onto him.

As if to rescue him from his dilemma, his shaft came erect with a vengeance. As it surged to life, she pulled quickly back and swung around to face him, her breasts dangling inches from his face. He took one of her nipples in his mouth, sucked on it, then lashed it with his tongue. She cried out softly, then gave him her other nipple. As his mouth closed about it, she reached back with one hand and guided his engorged shaft deep inside her.

With a sigh, she sat back, allowing him to range deep inside her.

"Now," she told him, her voice hushed, "lie still. Go to sleep if you want. I have what I want now."

Slowly, very slowly, she began to rock, occasionally rotating herself atop him to vary the rhythm, her pleasure obvious as she savored every stroke, her head flung back so that the line of her neck was taut, her black hair trailing so far back it covered Fargo's knees. Caught in her seductive rhythm, he lost all track of time. Indeed, for a second or two he seemed to have dozed off. But if he had, it was not for long.

She had increased the tempo, igniting a raging fire in his groin. He found himself slamming violently up to meet her every downward stroke. Her face had become a grim, taut mask, her mouth open as she flung her head from side to side, the black penumbra of her hair filling the air about her head. Tiny, barely audible grunts broke from her.

He began to cry out softly himself as they both built to their climax. When it came, he reached up and grabbed her with both arms, clasping her to him, then rolling her over. Once she was under him, he plunged in still deeper and kept on exploding—over and over.

At last he collapsed and rolled off her. She sat up, then got to her feet.

"Now," she said, "you can sleep."

He nodded lazily flung the soogan's flap over him and watched her climb back into her greasy deerskin dress. A moment later she had disappeared out the barn door, and he closed his eyes—totally exhausted.

Though he slept, it was a disturbed, restless sleep. He found himself caught in the coils of a nightmare and, struggling, managed to fling off the coils of the fiend pulling him to his death. He awoke with a sudden alert awareness of danger and saw Rawlinson's shadowy figure hovering over him. Rawlinson lifted his arm. Fargo caught the gleam of a knife.

A split second before it flashed down, Fargo rolled aside. The knife sliced through the soogan and bit deep into the floorboard beneath it. Fargo vaulted to his feet, caught Rawlinson in the midsection with his shoulder, and slammed him violently back against the stall. Rawlinson gasped in surprise and pain. Managing to twist out of Fargo's grasp, he turned to flee the barn. But Fargo caught him from behind, spun him back around, and flung him headfirst into the wall.

Rawlinson groaned, straightened, and turned groggily to face Fargo, both hands reaching up to protect himself. Fargo punched through the man's weak defense, catching him viciously on the chin, driving his head back against the wall. Boring in relentlessly, Fargo drove his right fist deep into the man's groin. Retching violently, Rawlinson collapsed to the floor. Fargo yanked the man back onto his feet, straightened him with another piledriver to the face, and kept after him. Punching now with metronomic precision, he snapped Rawlinson back against one of the pole's supporting the barn's roof.

The man cried out, then went slack.

Startled, Fargo stepped back as Rawlinson toppled forward onto a pile of hay. A bright beam of moonlight shining through the open barn door struck Rawlinson's back, revealing a small, ragged wound in the man's back. A dark stain was already spreading out from it, covering his filthy undershirt.

Glancing up at the post, Fargo saw the nail on which he had impaled Rawlinson. Fargo wanted to feel bad about it, but could not quite manage it.

A heavy figure appeared in the yard, hurrying toward the barn. It was Rawlinson's squaw, Mountain Flower. She was evidently coming to see what was taking her husband so long to dispatch their guest for the night. Fargo caught the gleam of Rawlinson's Hawken in the moonlight.

Fargo dragged Rawlinson out of the moonlight over to his soogan, then pulled Rawlinson's knife from the floorboard. A moment later Mountain Flower's bulk paused in the doorway, darkening the barn considerably.

"Hold it right there," Fargo told the woman. "I got this knife against your man's neck. Drop that rifle or I'll slit his throat."

She hesitated.

"I mean it!"

She let the rifle fall to the ground, then stepped back out of the doorway.

Fargo stepped over Rawlinson's body and picked up the Hawken. "He's in there on the floor," Fargo told Mountain Flower. "Maybe you better go in and see to him."

Suddenly Mary Jane materialized from the darkness. Uttering a keening war cry, she rushed him, a long blade in her hand. Fargo ducked and swung the Hawken's stock. It caught her on the side of the face and sent her tumbling backward, the knife flying from her hand. Sensing her opportunity, Mountain Flower came at Fargo. He ducked easily out of her lumbering path, and as she puffed, grunting, past him, he booted her ungallantly in the backside and sent her sprawling awkwardly into the side of the barn door. She struck it noisily, then slid down it to the doorsill, blinking up at him with her fathomless black eyes.

Fargo turned back to Mary Jane. She was up, holding the side of her face. A steady stream of blood was issuing from one nostril.

Fargo straightened himself wearily. Only now did he realize how wildly his head was throbbing, and he found himself sucking in deep gutfuls of air. He was sure as hell having a difficult time getting to sleep this night.

"Why don't you two stop all this nonsense?" Fargo suggested. "Your man is in there hurt bad. He's bleeding. If you don't take care of him, he won't be able to keep up this lovely ranch for you anymore."

Without a word the two women pushed themselves slowly onto their feet and moved past him into the barn. A moment later Mountain Flower, with Mary Jane beside her, emerged from the barn with Rawlinson in her arms and proceeded to carry him to the cabin. In her ample arms Rawlinson appeared no more substantial than an oversized rag doll.

Fargo got no more sleep that night. He sat up with his Sharps cradled in his arms until sunup, when Mary Jane came out to the barn to invite him in for breakfast. Fargo was so startled by the invitation that he accepted. He followed Mary Jane into the cabin and sat down, resting his Colt on the table beside him.

Rawlinson was sitting up in the far corner, a bandage wrapped tightly around his chest. He looked pale, but seemed reasonably fit, considering. He smiled slightly at Fargo.

"Sorry about all that jumpin' about last night," he managed, his voice soft. "But that other feller took my only hoss, and I sure could use that purty pinto of yours."

Fargo nodded. "You could have asked."

"You would have said no."

"That's right."

Mountain Flower put an enormous platter of ham and eggs, garnished with a small mountain of fried potatoes down in front of Fargo. Mary Jane poured his coffee and set that cheerfully before him, as well. Both of them seemed unperturbed at his presence, as if their concerted attempt to murder and dismember him the night before had been only a lighthearted game.

With a weary shrug, Fargo set to work on his breakfast. It was delicious, and both women watched him eat it with an almost fond regard.

After the breakfast, Fargo left the cabin and mounted up.

Mary Jane watched from the doorway. "No hard feelin's, Mr. Fargo," she said. "All we wanted was that hoss of yours. Like Pa said, it's right purty."

Fargo turned the pinto and allowed himself to smile back at her. "And all that last night was to get me real tired."

She nodded, almost shyly. "I guess maybe I left you too soon."

"Guess maybe you did at that," Fargo replied, setting his Ovaro on his way.

He looked back only once. Mountain Flower was standing beside Mary Jane, passing her the jug of moonshine. With Rawlinson laid up, those two were about to get all the firewater they wanted. Fargo chuckled at the thought.

Before nightfall, Rawlinson was going to have his hands full.

3

At sundown three days later, Fargo entered a high valley and saw, about a mile or so ahead of him, the dim cluster of buildings that was the town of Pine Bluff.

As he rode on toward the town, he approached a medium-sized herd of buffalo feeding on the thick, spongy grama grass that covered the valley floor. Most of the herd occupied the center of the valley, but some of the massive, hunched beasts were ranging far from the herd, feasting in the hollows on the tawny bluestem, some of it high enough to brush the belly of his pinto.

As Fargo rode close by one old bull, the big fellow turned to face him, lowered its head, and snorted some, its tiny ears fluttering. The pinto did not spook and Fargo kept to the same pace. A moment later the bull returned to his grazing.

Pine Bluff got its name, Fargo assumed, from the

pine-studded bluff that towered like a sentinel over it. Clattering across the rough-plank bridge spanning a shallow stream, Fargo saw that, of the half-dozen or so false-front stores lining both sides of the main street, a depressing number were out of business. The imposing brick hotel on the other end of town looked as if it had closed off its top third floor to guests. The shades in each of the windows were drawn and faded to a blank, staring white by the hot sun.

It was a town in trouble, obviously. The men lounging on the porch outside the town's only saloon reminded Fargo of vultures hunched on a tree branch. He rode on past the saloon without pause, feeling the eyes of the hard cases watching him. This town, more than likely, was where those driven from Deer Lodge had come to roost.

He kept on going until he reached the hotel. It was called the St. James. Dismounting stiffly, Fargo dropped his reins over the hitch rail and went inside. The desk clerk was a tall beanpole of a man with a prominent Adam's apple. He was dressed in an immaculate white cotton shirt and a dark frock coat. A black string tie was knotted at his throat.

Smoothing his thinning gray hair back needlessly with a long-fingered hand, he smiled cheerfully as Fargo approached the desk.

"Good afternoon, sir," he said in a clipped British accent. "A room for the night?"

Fargo nodded and signed the register. Then he looked up at the clerk. "Maybe you can tell me where I can get a bath nearby."

The clerk glanced down at the register. "You will

find a barbershop on the corner, Mr. Fargo," he said pleasantly. "The livery is at the rear of the hotel."

The clerk placed a brass key and tag down before Fargo. "Room fourteen. Second floor, rear."

Fargo dropped the key into his pocket and left the hotel, impressed in spite of himself. He was surprised to find such a well-constructed hotel—not to mention such a courteous and civil desk clerk—this high in the Rockies. He led his pinto around to the rear of the hotel and into the livery stable.

A young girl in her early twenties appeared at the foot of a stairway. She took the Ovaro from him with a smile.

"I'm Betty," she said. "My father and I run the hotel."

"Fargo," he told her. "Skye Fargo."

The girl was wearing Levi's and a red cotton shirt. She was almost as tall as Fargo, and her eyes and the shape of her face reminded him at once of the man who had checked him in. She would not have had to tell him that she was his daughter.

Fargo followed close behind her as she led the pinto into a stall. Her movements were deft and gentle as she lifted the saddle from the steaming pinto's back and sat it upon the stall's partition. Fargo stepped outside the stall, untied his saddle roll, and lifted the Sharps from its scabbard.

"He's had a long ride," Fargo told her. "Do your best for him."

"Of course," the girl replied. She was already reaching for the water bucket.

Burt Physer was the barber, a short jowly man

who was more than generous with the hot water he poured into Fargo's tub. After lazing in the tub for a full half-hour, Fargo dressed in fresh buckskins and let Burt shave him.

During the shave, Fargo got the story of the town.

The owner of the hotel was Ronald Burton. He and his daughter, Betty, ran the hotel alone. Burton had once been a high official of the Hudson Bay Company in Oregon. When the trapping in the region ran out, Burton conceived the notion of building a town that would become a jumping-off place for those settlers and prospectors pouring into California and Oregon in search of gold and farmland.

But the gold rush had long since petered out, and only a few settlers making the trek west knew of the town of Pine Bluff, so far off the Oregon Trail. Since Burton had sunk all his savings in the construction of his hotel and in aiding the construction of the other places of business, he was now stuck here in Pine Bluff, waiting and hoping for the influx of settlers he was still counting on to make his fortune.

Meanwhile, one of the general stores, a mill, and a blacksmith shop had been abandoned by their owners, leaving the town to exist on the revenue provided by the few settlers who did come through during the summer months and by an increasing number of hard cases that drifted into Pine Bluff in search of a haven from justice. The only money spent in Pine Bluff for the past month or so, Burt Physer maintained, came from stagecoach raises and other assorted villainies. A few of these rascals were not above trading liquor to the Nez Percé for horseflesh and young girls. The girls they used in the saloon, and the horseflesh they sold to ranchers farther south.

"I always can tell when someplace had a bank robbed or a stage held up," Burt said, stropping his razor. "Not long after, this here town gets wilder than a bronc with a burr under its saddle. On such holidays, it's worth your life to go outside. Lead fills the air as thick as mosquitoes at sundown."

The barber peeled the sheet off Fargo and snapped it for emphasis.

"Shave, haircut, and bath. That'll be two bits, mister."

Fargo dropped the coin into the barber's waiting palm. "I'm looking for a big redhead. Calls himself Red Ericson. He's got a woman with him."

The little man's face went grim. "I seen him, sure enough. But I don't want the pleasure a second time. Ask Ike Landusky. He owns the saloon. He'd know a lot more about him than me."

"Is Ericson still here?"

"Nope. He pulled out three days ago."

"Was there a woman with him?"

"He camped out of town. If he had a woman, I didn't see her."

"Thanks," Fargo said.

Physer cleared his throat. "You a bounty hunter, mister?"

Fargo shook his head and left the barbershop. He crossed the street and entered the hotel.

The girl was on the desk. She looked up brightly as he approached, and smiled. "If you're hungry," she said, "I'd be glad to fix something. We don't have a menu or anything, there are so few travelers this time of year."

"Steak and fixin's it'd be fine," Fargo told her.

"It won't take a minute. Go into the restaurant and find a table. Take any one at all. It doesn't matter."

He entered the small but immaculately kept restaurant and found a table near a window that offered a fine view of the bluff that towered over the town. The girl hurried over with silverware and fresh linen. As she poured a glass of water, he glanced up at her.

"Why not join me?" he said. "I'd sure appreciate the company. Your old man can hold down the front desk, can't he?"

She blushed. "If you wish."

"Fine."

The meal was served with astonishingly little delay. Its savory aroma inflamed his appetite as Betty placed it down before him. There was a platter holding an enormously thick steak, a bowl of mashed potatoes with plenty of rich gravy, a plate of thick-sliced bread still warm from the oven with a saucer of freshly churned butter. The steaming coffee had plenty of cream and honey to go with it. After Betty set a fresh pot of coffee down before him, she sat across from him, content with a modest portion of steak and half a baked potato.

Fargo asked her how she liked it up here in this high valley so far from civilization, helping to run a hotel that boasted so little traffic. She answered truthfully that at times she found it a little boring, adding that she found the winters the worst of all.

"I'm not looking forward to the next one," she admitted.

"Have those hard cases drifting in here given you much trouble?" Fargo asked, pouring a generous dollop of honey into his coffee.

"I stay away from the saloon," she admitted. "Even so, I am afraid sometimes—especially when I hear shooting late at night. It usually brings me fully awake. My father keeps a fully loaded shotgun at hand always."

"Doesn't sound very pleasant, at that."

She nodded thoughtfully. "Sometimes the Nez Percé come into town to trade—and to drink. At such times, when those poor Indians go crazy on all that liquor, I am almost convinced we have built this hotel on the outer fringes of hell."

"It must be lonely for you."

"It is. The Nez Percé braves—and these gun-toting barbarians do not excite my fancy. Indeed, Mr. Fargo, there is a decided lack of eligible males in this part of the world, I am afraid."

"I'm surprised you've stuck it out," Fargo remarked.

"My father and I have great confidence in this country, Mr. Fargo. It will not always be like this. Someday, instead of the buffalo, there will be cattle, instead of the Indians, settlers—the way it is in Oregon and California."

"I hope for your sake you're right."

She smiled wanly. "So do I, Mr. Fargo."

"Call me Skye," he said, smiling at her.

She blushed and nodded. Then, seeing that he had

finished, she excused herself, got up and began clearing off his table.

He bid her good night and left the hotel. In the gathering dusk, he paused on the hotel porch for a moment to get his bearings, then walked down the street past a small general store and the abandoned blacksmith's shop. Reaching the saloon, he tramped up onto the low porch and shouldered through the batwings and paused, aware of the hard faces that swung around to stare at him.

The saloon's floor was covered with sawdust that had not been swamped for weeks, and most of the cuspidors were overflowing with tobacco juice. Coils of smoke hung thickly in the sluggish air. The stench of unwashed feet and cheap cigars filled the place.

Three bar girls—dressed in short, faded blue dresses—turned in his direction. They were very young Indians girls. Nez Percé, he judged from the look of them. One of them was barely in her teens. More than likely they had been sold to the saloon's owner for not much more than cheap, rotgut whiskey—or a rifle and a few threadbare blankets. They looked drawn and forlorn, despite their gaudy attire, like children who had long since given up trying to escape a nightmare. One of them, the youngest, had stuck a wild flower in her hair. It had long since wilted.

As Fargo remained standing in the doorway, the silence became oppressive. He could hear clearly the sound of the batwings still flipping shut behind him. There was not a man in the place, he realized, who did not know why he was in Pine Bluff—or why he had just strode into this saloon. Fargo had given

Burt Physer all the time he needed to waddle across the street and spill everything he'd learned about Fargo to Ike Landusky.

Slowly, as if tired of the game, the gray, sullen faces turned their gaze away from Fargo. The low mutter of voices came again from every corner of the room, followed by the sharp clink of poker chips.

Fargo walked over to the bar. "Whiskey," he told the barkeep.

The barkeep slapped a bottle and a shot glass down on the bar. Fargo paid him and poured himself a drink, then took the bottle over to a table in the back of the saloon. He sat down with his back to the wall.

Fargo was able to pick out Landusky with little difficulty. Hearing the man being called Ike by his companions, he glanced over to see him playing poker at a table in the center of the room. Landusky was a powerful man with a raw face purpled from drink. His eyes were small and sharp, with a slightly yellow cast to them. When he spoke, it was like the bark of a sick animal. The men watching the poker game from the sidelines treated Landusky with such abject subservience that Fargo found it unpleasant to watch.

The saloon's patrons were a dirty and disheveled crew wearing a variety of costumes and hats of all shapes and sizes. The only clean and well-cared-for items on their persons were the gleaming six-guns strapped to their thighs. Gradually, as Fargo sipped his whiskey and studied their sodden faces and the slack emptiness in their eyes, he felt growing within him a bone-deep revulsion.

What most offended him, besides their blatant filthiness and their ugly, whiskey-fogged senses, was the crude and thoughtless way they handled the Indian girls. They fondled the girls openly, brutally, without shame, their hands groping clumsily, their bewhiskered faces rubbing heedlessly against the girls' silken cheeks.

These were not men, Fargo concluded. These were animals.

Fargo was reaching for his bottle when a sharp cry came from his right.

He turned in time to see a huge prospector cuff one of the girls on her cheek. The brutal force of the blow spun her head around. The girl closed her eyes and tried not to cry, though tears were already moving down her round dark cheeks. Then, her spirit broken, her lips compressed, she allowed the man to pull her back down onto his lap. She was the girl Fargo had noticed earlier, the one wearing the flower. It now looped sadly down over one ear.

"That's the way, Brad," someone shouted approvingly.

"You bet," the prospector growled, his rough bark of laughter cutting through the saloon.

The man looked as if he had just come in from working a claim. His clothes were plastered with dried mud, and even his stocking cap was thick with mire. Most of his face was covered by a coal-black beard. Small, bright-blue eyes peered hungrily at the girl, who could not have been more than twelve. Reaching his big hand around her waist, the prospector grabbed one of her tiny breasts and squeezed. The girl started to struggle slightly, but again she was brought to heel with a quick, powerful slap. All resistance crumbled. The girl bowed her head and submitted meekly to the prospector's rough, unfeeling pawing.

Unable to conceal his distaste any longer, Fargo got to his feet, his eyes fixed coldly on the man. The prospector glanced quickly up at him, his heavy face twisting into a snarl.

"What the hell you lookin' at, sonny?" he barked arrogantly.

"I was just wondering," Fargo said easily, softly.

At once the place went deathly quiet. Ike Landusky put down his poker hand and turned to watch.

"Wonderin' what?" the prospector demanded.

"Why a big slob like you can only make it with little girls."

The prospector got to his feet so suddenly the chair he was sitting on went over onto his back. Fargo smiled at him. The man pulled up in some confusion.

Fargo's quiet, stinging insult had easily carried the length of the saloon. In the shocked, waiting silence that now followed, Fargo strode casually over to the prospector's table, took the girl's arm, and pulled her gently toward him. Escorting her a few feet from the prospector's table, he then pushed her safely out of the way, smiling at her as he did so. The girl turned and darted toward one of the other girls.

"You goin' to let him get away with that, Brad?" Landusky growled.

"Hell, no," the prospector said, pushing the table aside and lunging toward Fargo.

"Go get him, Poucher," someone yelled.

Pulling up in front of Fargo, Brad Poucher swung on him. It was a wild, roundhouse blow that caught nothing but air. Fargo ducked, then stepped in close and slapped the bearded prospector sharply on the side of his face.

"How's that feel?" Fargo inquired, ducking easily back out of the man's reach.

Then he let his right hand drop to his Colt.

Brad pulled up suddenly, breathing heavily, his beady eyes narrowing. For the first time, it seemed, he became aware of the icy, murderous look in Fargo's lake-blue eyes.

"Is that what yer after?" Poucher demanded. "You callin' me?"

Fargo replied softly, "Whatever's your pleasure."

Things were happening a little too fast for Poucher's whiskey-befogged senses to comprehend. But one thing he knew: Fargo would be no pushover. Nevertheless, he had just been called. He had no choice.

His hand dropped to his holster.

Fargo placed his foot against the table and jammed it into Poucher's midsection, driving him back violently. The table's edge almost cut him in half as it jammed him against the wall. Poucher gasped painfully and dropped his gun.

Reaching over with both hands, Fargo yanked the man out from behind the table and flung him bodily across the saloon. Poucher spun once, lost his balance, and reeled backward into the bar. As he tried to catch himself, his big feet got tangled in the foot rail and he went down heavily on his back. Before he could recover, Fargo strode over and stomped on his right wrist. The sound of the bones crunching under his heel filled the shocked saloon. As the big prospector, writhing in agony, clung to his shattered wrist, Fargo turned to face the others.

Terrified, the bar girls were now huddled in a corner. Every man was on his feet, crouching slightly, gun hands hovering over gun butts. Fargo straightened, animated by a mean eagerness to cut a bloody swath through this miserable pack.

"Okay," he said softly. "Which one of you wants to be next?"

Landusky spoke first. "Who the hell are you, mister?"

"You know who I am. Burt Physer told you. And you know why I'm in Pine Bluff."

His yellow eyes gleaming shrewdly, Landusky said, "Sure, Burt told us. But I don't know nothin' about this feller Ericson you're lookin' for. My advice to you is ride out. While you still can."

"After what I just done to your friend here?"

"We ain't got no quarrel with you, Fargo. We all saw what happened. Brad started the whole thing." Landusky glanced quickly about him. "Ain't that right, fellers?"

"Sure," the one nearest Landusky agreed. The rest nodded. But they were still crouched and their hands still hovered only inches above their six-guns.

Fargo smiled tightly and waited. It didn't take long. Landusky's hand dropped toward his gun. Fargo was so quick his Colt seemed to have materialized in his hand.

Still in the act of drawing, Ike found himself peering into the muzzle of Fargo's six-gun. His face went slack. He was about ready to piss in his pants out of sheer terror. Those standing close beside him straightened up and lifted their hands away from their weapons. Then they moved hastily aside. Landusky let his Colt drop back into his holster.

"Easy, now, Fargo," he said. "I ain't goin' for my weapon. You can see that clear."

"Where's Red Ericson?"

"I told you. I don't know nothing about him."

Fargo thumb-cocked his Colt and lowered the barrel so that it was trained on Landusky's crotch.

The man swallowed. Beads of cold sweat stood out on his white face. "All right," he cried hastily. "So Red *was* here. But he left three days ago."

"Where'd he go?"

"He didn't tell me. Honest, Fargo. Besides, I ain't his keeper."

Out of the corner of his eye, Fargo saw the barkeep's shoulder dip as he reached for his sawed-off shotgun under the counter.

Fargo swung his gun around and fired. The man's face became a bloody hole a second before it vanished. His shotgun clattered across the polished surface of the bar and crashed to the floor. Fargo turned back around. A small, ferret-faced man had drawn his gun. He fired hastily. As the slug shattered the bar mirror behind him, Fargo fired back—twice.

Both slugs caught the little man squarely in his chest, slamming him sharply back against a table. Dropping his gun, the fellow collapsed slowly forward onto another table, rolled off it, and thudded heavily to the floor.

Not a man moved to help him. Through the thick

clouds of white, acrid smoke, Fargo leveled his six-gun on Landusky.

"I'm going to ask you one more time, Landusky," Fargo told him. "Where's Ericson?"

Landusky moistened his lips and tried not to look at the muzzle of Fargo's gun. "Red's at Willow Pass. He's got a cabin there on the creek. He said he's plannin' on wintering there. Jesus Christ, Fargo! He'll kill me for tellin' you."

"I don't see you had much choice in the matter," Fargo replied, studying the man curiously. "But why in the hell should you care about him?"

"Because the crazy son of a bitch is my step-brother."

"I wouldn't be proud of that, Landusky."

"Who says I am?"

His six-gun still covering Landusky, Fargo strode carefully from the saloon. When he reached the door and stepped out into the chill night, he heard the rush of feet approaching the door behind him. He turned and fired two quick shots through the batwings. The rush halted and the saloon became very still.

Someone crouching near the door cursed softly, bitterly.

As Fargo entered the hotel a few minutes later, Ronald Burton glanced up to greet him, a smile on his face. He had been in the act of putting away the register.

"Would you ask Betty to saddle my horse?" Fargo asked him. "It looks like I won't be stayin' for the night, after all. Too bad. I was lookin' forward to clean sheets."

"Trouble, Mr. Fargo?"

"Not if I can get my ass out of here fast enough. Think you can keep Landusky's pack at bay for a while?"

The man's eyes lit at the prospect. "You may go up to your room in perfect confidence," he said, hauling a sawed-off shotgun up from behind the counter.

He tapped the bell and Betty appeared in the doorway. As Burton told her what Fargo wanted, Fargo hurried up the stairs to his room. Once inside the room, he shoved a chair under the doorknob, then reloaded his Colt. Then he bunched up the bedclothes expertly and stepped back to inspect his handiwork. He was pleased. In the bright moonlight filtering in through the window, anyone entering his room would think he was fast asleep.

He removed his bottle of bourbon from the saddlebag, unstoppered it, and took a healthy belt. Then he replaced the bottle and walked over to the window. As he had determined earlier, the roof of the hotel livery was just under it.

Leaving enough silver on the dresser to take care of his bill, he gathered up his Sharps and the rest of his gear and climbed out onto the roof. Lowering the window carefully behind him, he moved to the edge of the roof and dropped lightly to the ground.

Betty was waiting in the livery entrance with his pinto already saddled. As she watched silently, he dropped the Sharps into the scabbard, then tied his bedroll and saddlebags securely behind the saddle.

Taking the reins from her, he stepped into the saddle.

"Which way's Willow Pass, Betty?"

"Go north, straight to the end of this valley. Head for the Twin Peaks. Willow Pass is on the other side."

"Thanks. Tell your father to put away that shotgun now. No need to stir up a hornet's nest. I'm safely on my way."

"I'm sorry you are going so soon," she told him, her upturned face pale in the moonlight.

"I'll be back," he told her without much conviction.

"I hope so, Skye Fargo."

With a wave, he nudged the Ovaro's flanks lightly and rode into the night. He kept to the alley that ran behind the hotel until he was quit of the town. Then he lifted the pinto to a lope and made for the dim, hulking bulk of the pine bluff filling the night sky ahead of him.

Cresting the bluff finally after a tough climb, he pulled the pinto around to let him blow. As far as the eye could see, the valley was spread out before him, its sea of grass almost blue in the moonlight's bright wash. Just beneath the pinto's hooves, he could see Pine Bluff's pathetic cluster, the buildings' roofs and sides silvered in the moonlight.

Frowning, he peered more closely down at the buildings. He thought he heard the faint staccato of gunfire. Then the breeze shifted and with it went all sound from that direction. Fargo sat his horse patiently. He knew that once Landusky found out Fargo had already fled, he would send a rider to warn Ericson.

Fargo did not have long to wait.

A lone rider galloped out of town. In the bright moonlight Fargo could see him clearly. As soon as he left Pine Bluff, he did not ride north toward Willow Pass, where Ericson was supposed to be holed up. Instead, he turned his mount sharply and rode due west, heading across the valley toward a heavily wooded tableland lifting darkly into the night sky.

Fargo chuckled. He was not the least bit surprised.

Nudging the pinto off the bluff, he angled down the slope, his gaze fastened on the rider who was going to lead him to Red Ericson.

4

Red Ericson pulled back suddenly and looked down at the girl. She had allowed him to spread her legs apart, but she remained as rigid as a board. He had only to mount and thrust home to take her. But he missed her usual screams, her fierce, dogged struggle. He looked down into her eyes. She stared back up at him. But it was clear she did not see him. A coldness seeped into his bones. He rolled off her and got to his feet.

"Hey, Cindy," he said, "what's the matter? Ain't you gonna give me some fight this time?"

She did not respond. She remained on her back, as still and unyielding as a corpse. Shuddering inwardly, he reached for his pants and stepped into them, watching her all the while.

Earlier, when he had first abducted her, she had lapsed into similar silences. Most of the time since, however, she had just cried bitterly, sometimes railing at him, at other times pleading with him to let her go as he had promised. But this new wrinkle—this vacant, fathomless look in her eyes—had lasted some time now, and he was beginning to wonder how long it would go on. Not much longer, he hoped. He was getting sick of her crouching in the corner of the cabin, staring straight ahead at nothing. He needed her to cook for him, to take care of the place, and especially to help in skinning and dressing the few beaver he was bringing in.

He bent suddenly close to her and peered once more down into her eyes. The expression on her face did not change. Was she faking it? he wondered. He stared down at her a moment longer. Then, with a shrug, he straightened and looked out the cabin's single boarded window.

It was not yet dark, still early enough for him to check his traps along the river. He put on his deer-skin jacket and walked over to the wall where his rifle and gear were hung. He was reaching for the rifle when he heard an inarticulate cry behind him.

Turning, he was only just in time to catch Cindy by the wrist as she stabbed downward with his long skinning knife, her face contorted with rage. Though he was far stronger, the suddenness of her attack and the ungovernable fury that drove her imparted a fierce strength to her thrust. The blade of the knife broke through his guard and slice into a portion of his left shoulder.

Ignoring the superficial wound, he closed his right fist about her wrist until her face contorted in pain and she let the knife drop from her fingers. He slapped her. Hard. Her face snapped around. Then he punched her. His blood up now, he kept after her, driving her before him. The lightning-swift flurry of blows that caught her about the face and head was soon all that was keeping her up. Only when the back of her knees struck the edge of the cot did she go down.

This time, with a wild, uncaring ferocity, he took her.

She was staring up at the ceiling, her face and her entire body rigid, when he pulled back and left her. He reached once again for his rifle and stepped out of the cabin. Outside, he dropped the thick beam in place across the door, locking her in. She had tried to run away so often, this had become a precaution of his whenever he left for any length of time.

Somewhat unsettled, Ericson walked toward the stream below the cabin. The water shimmered in the late-afternoon sunlight. As he strode through the pines bordering the stream, a storm of raucous blackbirds rose in a dark cloud. He paid them no heed.

Despite himself, he was thinking of the girl. But why? He had what he wanted. He could take her whenever he wanted. Yet, this thought did not comfort him. Abruptly, he pulled up and turned to look back at the cabin. He knew what was bothering him! For some crazy reason he couldn't figure, he wanted the girl to *want* him—to struggle, sure, but only just long enough to give it some spice. After that, he wanted her to join in with him completely.

Shaking his head at this silly, monumental foolishness, he turned about and resumed his walk to the stream.

"Red!"

Ericson glanced to his right. A rider was emerging from the timber bordering the stream. Pete Quinlan. The Irishman's huge sombrero was instantly recognizable—that and his tattered gray poncho. As Quinlan cut across the flat toward him, Ericson saw that the man's square face was weary and lined, his brows covered with sweat-caked grime. The bay he was riding looked about done in. Streaks of dried lather laced its chest.

Pulling to a halt beside Ericson, Quinlan dismounted stiffly. "Ike sent me, Red."

"Goddammit! I told that foolish son of a bitch not to tell anyone where I was holing up."

"I know that, Red. But, hell, I ain't goin' to tell anyone."

Ericson looked at Quinlan for a long, frustrating minute, then realized it would do no good to argue with the poor sap. He was only doing what Ike had told him to do.

"All right," he asked angrily. "What's this all about? What's Ike want?"

"He don't want nothin', Red. He sent me to warn you. There's someone on your tail."

Red's eyes narrowed. "Who?"

"Name's Skye Fargo. He shot up Ike's saloon—killed two men and messed up Brad somethin' fierce. He's a bear of a man once he gets his dander up."

Ericson felt a momentary qualm. He thought he had sent a slug into Fargo when he burst into the saloon. That was who he had been aiming at. But he could have hit the sheriff instead, which was why it was Fargo and not Wills on his tail. And he guessed if he had a choice in the matter, he would feel a mite easier with Wills on his tail instead of Fargo.

"But you don't have to worry none, Red," Quinlan said. "Ike told him you was at Willow Pass."

"That so? And you think this guy Fargo would believe what Ike told him?"

"Sure, Red."

Ericson shook his head in disgust. "You're a fool, Quinlan. Do you know that?"

Quinlan shifted his feet. Ericson's ridicule was not easy to take, but just this once, he seemed to be telling himself, he would take it.

Red sighed. Then he peered carefully at Quinlan. "Now, you think back, Pete. Think real hard. Are you *sure* no one followed you here?"

Quinlan looked suddenly uneasy. "I don't think so, Red."

"You don't think so? Damn it to hell! You mean you're not sure?"

Quinlan cowered before Ericson's fury. "I'm pretty sure I wasn't, Red," he protested. "There was just one time when I thought maybe I caught a movement on the trail behind me, but I pulled up and rode back a ways and there weren't nothin' there."

"Shit! You mean the son of a bitch tailin' you kept his head down when you went lookin' for him. All right, Quinlan. Go on back to Pine bluff. I should've known better than to tell Ike where I was headin'."

"Jesus, Red. I can't ride back now. I been travelin' for two days and two nights. I'm plumb wore out. Couldn't I light and set a spell?" He glanced toward the cabin. "I could sure use some coffee."

"No."

"That ain't very neighborly, Red."

Ericson cocked his rifle and poked the muzzle into Quinlan's gut. "I ought to've shot you out of the saddle when you rode in here. You and Ike've done give me away. Go on! Git, before I blow your balls clear across this here field."

Quinlan wasted no time climbing back into his saddle. With brutal haste, he hauled back on his dun's reins and wheeled the animal about. A moment later he had disappeared at full gallop back into the timber.

Ericson turned and hurried back to the cabin. Bursting in, he peered into the sudden gloom. The girl was still on the bed where he had left her. But now she was sitting up with her back to the wall. Like a wild, frightened animal, she peered in his direction.

"I'll be comin' back for you later," he told her coldly, his voice deliberately harsh. "And this time you're goin' to make me real happy."

Her eyes burned like embers as she contemplated him. For a moment he thought she was going to hurl herself across the room at him. Chuckling meanly, he uncocked his loaded Colt and tossed it lightly onto the bed. She pounced on it. But before she could raise it to fire, he stepped back out through the door and slammed it. Dropping the beam in place, he hurried up the slope behind the cabin.

Smiling at the cunning of the trap he had just set, Ericson was almost grateful to Ike and that fool Irishman he had sent to warn him.

Fargo moved as silently as a cat along the ledge

above the rider. A thick branch came between them. Fargo kept going past it, then launched himself. He struck the sombrero off the rider's head and flung a forearm around his neck as they both tumbled off his horse. When they struck the rocky trail, the rider managed to break loose. Slithering back along the ground, he clawed frantically for his six-gun.

Before he could bring it up, Fargo stepped forward and kicked the weapon from his grasp. The Colt vanished into the brush off the trail.

Fargo bent, grabbed the man's shirt front, and hauled him to his feet. Then he buried his fist deep into the man's gut. Doubling over, the fellow tried to spin away. But Fargo kept after him. Cuffing him smartly on the side of the head, he knocked him sharply back against a wall of rock. His head snapped back, the crack sounding sharply.

Slowly, the man sagged to the ground and came to rest with his back against the rock, his feet spread out on the ground before him. Dazedly, he stared up at Fargo. Once he had gotten close enough, Fargo had recognized the man instantly. He was one of the men crowding around Ike Landusky's poker table.

"What do they call you?" Fargo asked, stepping back.

The man moistened his lips and wiped off his face with the back of his hand. "Pete Quinlan," he mumbled.

"And I'm sure you know who I am."

"Yeah. Skye Fargo. You're the son of a bitch who shot up the saloon. You killed Sammy Newton and the barkeep."

"Don't forget that child molester, Brad."

"He'll get you. He swears it."

Fargo laughed.

"What . . . what're you goin' to do to me?"

"Use you to catch a skunk."

Quinlan stared sullenly up at Fargo. "Make sense, damn you."

"You just came back from seeing Ericson." Fargo told him. "Ike sent you to warn him. Right?"

The man nodded grudgingly. "I reckon."

"So you just saw Ericson."

Quinlan didn't bother to deny it.

"Did you see the girl with him?"

"Didn't see no girl."

Fargo frowned. "Has Red got himself a cabin?"

Quinlan nodded.

"Did you go inside?"

"No."

"After that long a ride he didn't invite you in?"

"No, he didn't."

Fargo considered that reply. Ericson was evidently intent on keeping Cindy out of sight. Fargo didn't like the sound of that. She was virtually a prisoner. He probably locked her in whenever he left to go anywhere. She was undoubtedly in the cabin now. And close by it—as a result of Quinlan's warning—Red Ericson was more than likely waiting for Fargo to show.

"Stand up," Fargo told Quinlan, covering him with his Colt. "Get your hat and follow me."

Quinlan struggled to his feet. He teetered uncertainly for a moment until he got his balance. Then, leading his horse, he walked ahead of Fargo back along the trail until they came to the spot where Fargo had tethered his pinto.

"All right, Quinlan," Fargo said, reaching into his saddle back for two strips of rawhide. "Mount up."

Quinlan did as he was told. Swiftly, Fargo bound Quinlan's feet to the stirrups and his hands to the saddle horn. Then Fargo mounted his pinto, and the two men rode back along the trail, Fargo leading Quinlan's dun.

"Where we heading?" Quinlan asked nervously.

"Back to Ericson's place."

"He knows you're coming. I warned him."

"That's what I'm counting on."

About a half-hour later, Fargo saw the flat through the timber and pulled Quinlan's horse to a halt. Dismounting, he untied Quinlan.

"Get down," he told Quinlan. "And take off your sombrero and the poncho."

"What the hell you up to, Fargo?"

"Just shut up and do as I tell you."

Quinlan dismounted, then dropped the sombrero and poncho to the ground beside Fargo. Fargo handed Quinlan his own hat, then peeled off his buckskin shirt and gave it to Quinlan also. "Put these on. Then get up onto my pinto."

Quinlan was not dumb. He saw at once what Fargo was planning. "Hey, now listen . . ."

Fargo pointed his Colt at Quinlan and cocked it. "Do as I say."

Reluctantly, Quinlan shrugged into Fargo's buckskin shirt, put on Fargo's hat, then climbed into the pinto's saddle. The Ovaro did not seem to like his new rider. Maybe it was the smell, Fargo thought.

As the animal snorted and moved skittishly, Fargo took his halter and talked softly to him, then patted his neck. As soon as the pinto quieted down, Fargo mounted Quinlan's dun, then pulled up behind Quinlan.

"Move out," he told Quinlan. "And ride across the flat directly to the cabin."

Quinlan turned his head to look at Fargo, his face pale. "Red'll think I'm you. You're goin' to make him shoot me instead of you."

Fargo waggled his Colt. "No more palaver. Move out!"

"It won't work. I'll make a break for it."

"Do that and I'll back-shoot you and take my chances. And if you were in Ike's saloon, you shouldn't doubt my word."

"I don't, you bastard."

"Then I ain't goin' to tell you again," Fargo said, thumb-cocking his Colt.

Quinlan looked back around and kicked his heels into the pinto's flank. A moment later they left the timber, rode for a short distance alongside the stream, then cut across the flat, heading for the cabin. As he got to within a hundred yards of it, he pulled the poncho closer up around his neck and tugged the brim of the sombrero farther down over his face.

Towering over the cabin was a steep, wooded slope. The cabin itself was a flimsy structure. Warped, weathered boards were slapped hastily over the frame, with little overlap and no real attempt to make the walls solid. The horse barn and corral behind it appeared to have been much more carefully constructed.

By that time, Fargo was close enough to see that a beam had been set in place across the doorway. He had been right. Cindy was imprisoned within the cabin. At once Fargo began inspecting the slope above the cabin. He had never expected to fool Ericson completely. The most this flimsy ruse could give him was time, during which Ericson might be lured into revealing his position.

Abruptly, a shot rang out from the slope above the cabin. Quinlan sagged forward, then pitched off the pinto. At once the pony bolted back the way they had come.

Letting it go, Fargo spurred his mount toward the slope. He had caught the flash of gunpowder on a ledge marked by a tall pine. At the moment, as he rode hard for the slope, he was still counting on Quinlan's sombrero and poncho to confuse Ericson.

But before he reached the slope, Ericson fired again. The round caught the dun in the chest. As the animal crashed to the ground, Fargo was thrown clear. Another round exploded in the ground inches from his head. Colt in hand, he scrambled to his feet and raced for cover on the slope. Once in the timber, he raced up the slope. A good distance up the slope, he broke into a clearing and glanced up through the trees. The tall pine was still visible, off to his right. He concentrated then on clawing up the steep, needle-slick ground.

He was about fifteen yards below the ledge when he saw Ericson through the pines. The man was down on one knee, his rifle up to his shoulder. He was sighting down the slope at Fargo. Fargo flung himself to one side just as Ericson fired.

The slug clipped a pine cone over Fargo's head. As the seeds showered him, Fargo flung his Colt up and squeezed off a shot. The rifle in Ericson's hand bucked violently upward, then disintegrated as Fargo's slug severed the stock from the barrel. Ericson was knocked back out of sight.

Scrambling up the slope after him, Fargo reached the ledge in time to see Ericson ducking behind a tree ten feet away. Fargo snapped off two quick shots. One slug gouged a chunk of bark out of the tree; the other whined off a boulder beyond it. Fargo usually hit what he aimed at, but he was winded from the long climb, and there was really no sense, he realized, in trying to shoot a man he could no longer see.

Holding his fire, he raced toward the tree. Just before he reached it, Ericson left it, heading for a stand of timber beyond. Fargo's Colt thundered. Ericson spun to the ground, his right hand grabbing at his side. But almost at once he was on his feet again, and a second later he disappeared into the brush.

Fargo slipped into the timber after Ericson. Though the man was wounded, he was as big as a bear and as dangerous as any cornered animal. Fargo heard a twig snap to his left and went that way. Pushing a low-hanging bough out of his path, he crossed a small, moss-covered clearing—and through a thicket to another clearing.

He pulled up and looked around. The pines were still. Even the wind seemed to be holding off, as if it, too, were waiting. Fargo thought he caught a flash of movement to his right and spun in that direction. He was just in time to see the erect tail of a chipmunk as the tiny rodent fled up a tree.

From behind him came the sound of branches parting. Fargo whirled. Rushing upon him like an enraged grizzly, Ericson bowled into Fargo, knocking him violently back. Fargo's foot caught a root and he went down heavily, just in time to escape the swift arc of Ericson's knife. The Colt was jarred from Fargo's grasp. Before he could pick it up, Ericson was on him again. Fargo straightened and managed to fling Ericson to the ground.

Ericson came down heavily in a patch of brush, but regained his feet with the speed of a cat and once again rushed Fargo. By this time, Fargo had drawn his bowie. He slipped to one side, slashing out at Ericson as the man lunged past. His blade sliced a neat line across the coiled, rust-colored hair that matted Ericson's chest.

Ericson's wild eyes lit with pain, but it did not slow him as he lunged forward again, slashing viciously at Fargo. Still on one knee, Fargo parried the lunge awkwardly. This time Ericson's blade sliced his left shoulder, but not deeply.

Fargo slashed up at Ericson, his blade cutting through muscle and grating against bone. A neat slice of Ericson's right thigh peeled off, a freshet of blood following out after it. With a grunt of both pain and surprise, Ericson turned and bolted back through the pines, Fargo right behind him.

It was a bad move on Ericson's part. Before he could get any distance between himself and Fargo, he was forced to pull up, trapped, on the ledge's rocky lip. He spun, crouching, to face Fargo.

Fargo slowed, then advanced cautiously, his feet spread wide, the tip of his knife tracing a tiny circle in the air in front of him. He kept his weight forward on the front of his toes and held his body as far back as possible. The flesh wound in his shoulder was entirely forgotten now.

Ericson's appearance gave Fargo grim comfort. His shirt hung from his frame, revealing a chest shining with blood, and the gaping thigh wound was bleeding freely. The loss of blood already appeared to have affected him. His face was deathly pale, his eyes narrowed with pain and concentration.

Fargo lunged; Ericson parried. Ericson lunged; Fargo parried. Like two fencers with truncated swords, they thrust and parried, circling each other warily. Soon their clothes were hanging in bloody strips as each serpent-like flick of the other's knife found its mark. Scores of lacerations, each oozing fresh red tongues of blood, appeared on their arms and torsos.

At last Ericson was forced to slump to one knee, his face drawn and pale from loss of blood. Sensing his opportunity, Fargo rushed him. Ericson saw him coming and dropped hastily back.

Fargo pulled up. Ericson—a terrified look on his face—was teetering on the brink of the ledge. Then, with a startled cry, he lost his balance, toppled backward, and vanished.

Fargo stepped closer to the lip of the ledge and looked over. Somehow, Ericson had managed to grab hold of a juniper root about ten feet below the ledge.

It was almost a sheer drop from that point, and Ericson was scrambling desperately to gain a foothold. Fargo smiled and prepared to climb down. Two swift slices from his Bowie would sever Ericson from that tree root.

Ericson, straining desperately to hang on, saw Fargo begin his descent.

"You son of a bitch!" he cried.

Fargo did not bother to reply as he descended to within a few feet of the juniper. When he reached down with his blade, Ericson, still cursing, let go. Despite his frantic efforts to grab hold of another tree or projection farther down, he began to tumble faster and faster down the slope until he disappeared. A moment later, Fargo heard him crashing heavily down through heavy brush.

Fargo climbed back up to the ledge and went back into the timber for his Colt. He doubted Ericson could have survived such a plunge, but he was determined to go down there and make sure.

A half-hour later, Fargo had still not found Ericson. He had discovered the spot where the man's heavy body landed finally, a blood-slicked tangle of scrub pine and juniper. Ericson's weight had almost flattened the brush. From there, the man's bloody trail led across the slope, then disappeared into the timber.

Now, deep in the timber, Fargo pulled up, suddenly alarmed. The woods were silent. There were no bird calls, no chatter from squirrels or woodchucks. The wary, waiting silence of the many woodland creatures who dwelt in this fragrant patch of timber told Fargo that Ericson had already smashed through here. But he could not follow the man any farther. Ericson's astonishing capacity to absorb punishment had already drawn Fargo too far from the cabin. Cindy was still back there in the cabin—her prison.

He turned and hurried back down through the timber, emerging less than fifty yards from the cabin. Dusk had fallen over the flat by this time. With no more than a glance at Quinlan's dead horse and Quinlan's sprawled body a short distance from the cabin, Fargo hurried to the door, lifted the beam, and pulled it open.

Ducking his head, he stepped into the cabin. A dim, smoky coal-oil lamp was burning on a table by the door. Squinting through the smoke, Fargo thought he saw Cindy sitting up on the bed. As he started toward her, he saw her hand go up and caught the gleam of a gun barrel. Before he could duck back, the revolver detonated.

The sudden detonation shook the tiny cabin. Something hot and enormously heavy struck Fargo on the side of the head. He felt himself lurching forward. As he slammed into the floor, he could feel the blood pouring down over his forehead and heard the squeak of the bedsprings as Cindy sprang to her feet and rushed at him.

Though he remained conscious, he could not move an inch. He was paralyzed. Then came a cry that chilled Fargo to the bone. It was followed by a second thunderous detonation. The floor inches in front of his face erupted in splinters. Another roar followed.

This time Fargo felt as well as heard it burrow into the floorboard near his right side.

"Here now," cried Ericson. "Let me have that."

Fargo heard Ericson's heavy feet tramping on the floorboards and then the sound of his rough palm slapping Cindy. The girl screamed, then grunted as Ericson struck her again. It sounded like a punch to her midsection. He heard Cindy sucking in her breath in agonized gulps. Fargo heard Ericson's hoarse chuckle.

"You killed him for me, woman. Just like I planned it. You killed the poor son of a bitch come to save you."

Cindy moaned, then cried out something unintelligible.

Again Fargo heard the sound of a struggle. This time it ended outside the cabin as Cindy's high shriek turned into a pitiful moan. A moment later Ericson reentered the cabin.

Fargo tried desperately to move, but still not a muscle responded. All the lines were down. Ericson paused in front of the table just in front of Fargo. Fargo heard Ericson strike a match, then became aware of Ericson bending over him. He heard the man's chuckle again. By this time the blood had matted in his hair and was flowing thickly down over his face, nearly blinding him.

Ericson straightened up. "Now, you son of a bitch," he cried hoarsely, "on your way to hell you're going to burn."

As he spoke, Ericson flung the lighted lamp to the floor. It struck just in front of Fargo's head, the flaming oil spilling away from Fargo, licking hungrily toward the wall.

Ericson watched for a moment, then stepped back and slammed shut the cabin door. Fargo heard the beam drop into place. The flames began racing up the walls. Thick, acrid smoke stung Fargo's eyes and seared his lungs. Above the roar of the flames, he heard dimly the sound of horses behind the cabin, moving off.

Fargo knew then how neatly Ericson had finessed him. Ericson had given Cindy a gun, knowing that when Fargo entered the cabin, she would fire upon him—thinking it was Ericson. The man must have primed her, goaded her, before locking her in with a loaded gun.

Fargo cursed bitterly—and heard his own voice! Groaning, he found that he could move, that he could lift himself onto his elbows. He reached up and felt of his head wound: a deep, bloody furrow that creased the side of his skull. The slug had rung his bell and maybe cracked his skull some, but it had not broken through.

Stumbling to his feet, he shielded his face with his forearm and turned to look for a window. The only one he saw was boarded up. The heat was building rapidly. The skin on the back of his neck was blistering. His buckskin pants were smoking, the fringes glowing. Even his boots were on fire, it seemed, and he was having difficulty keeping his eyes open.

Ducking low, he crawled away from the worst part of the fire and wedged himself into the corner between the fireplace and the wall. A blazing beam crashed to the floor beside him and he pushed back to escape its flames. The flimsy boards at his back gave slightly under his weight. At once, he planted both feet on the floor and heaved backward. The dry, weathered boards cracked, but did not give way. He thrust backward again. This time the weathered boards snapped, spilling Fargo out onto the blessedly cool grass.

As rapidly as he could, he crawled away from the flaming cabin toward a nearby clump of juniper. Behind him he heard a sudden roar as the cabin's roof collapsed. He reached the junipers with his buckskin leggings still smoking, and the back of his neck as raw as rare beefsteak. Struggling through the bushes, he sprawled into a shallow depression half-filled with ground water.

Gratefully, he sank into the water and the soft mud, allowing it to cover him almost completely, cooling his blistering skin, extinguishing at last his smoking leggings and fiery boots . . .

5

As soon as he was able, Fargo pushed himself upright and crossed the flat to the stream. In the chill air, he stripped himself and plunged into the icy waters, cleansing himself vigorously, his bloodied head especially. The cold water took much of the sting out of the myriad slashes and lacerations that covered his arms and chest. When he waded out of the water finally, his body tingled deliciously and his head had cleared considerably.

Pulling on his long johns, he walked into the timber in search of the pinto. He trusted the Ovaro not to have strayed far and was not disappointed. He found the pony on the edge of a small clearing, calmly cropping the lush grass it had found there. He led the pony back out through the timber, dressed in clean buckskins he took from his saddle roll, then mounted up and rode back to the smoldering cabin.

He wanted his hat and the buckskin shirt he had forced Quinlan to wear.

Quinlan's body was sprawled facedown in the tall grass, not twenty feet from the cabin. Fargo dismounted and picked up his hat, then approached the body. Judging from the dark slick of blood on the grass behind him, Quinlan had dragged himself a considerable distance before giving out. He was still enough now, however. Fargo felt a slight twinge of guilt for his part in Quinlan's violent demise.

Dropping to one knee beside the body, Fargo gently rolled the dead man over. But Quinlan was not dead. His eyes wide, he stared up at Fargo in a lunatic fury. Before Fargo could pull back, Quinlan's right hand lunged upward. Fargo felt a sharp, electrifying pain. He flung himself back, then staggered to his feet. The hilt of Quinlan's knife was protruding from his side. He wrenched the knife out and flung it away, the action sending a blaze of pain up his left side. A cold sweat broke out on his forehead and he suddenly felt as weak as a kitten.

"Knew you'd be back for your shirt," Quinlan told him, his voice barely audible. "See you soon, you bastard, in hell!"

Fargo did not respond. He was too busy tightening his belt around the wound in an effort to stanch the flow of blood. Quinlan began to cough. Then his head lolled loosely to one side. Fargo peered down at him. Quinlan's eyes were still open, but they saw nothing.

He was dead. Finally.

Despite himself, Fargo felt a grudging respect for the man as he knelt beside him and stripped his buckskin shirt from him. This done, he wound the shirt around his waist, tightened it by tying together the arms, then hauled himself up into his saddle.

Once astride the pinto, he had to wait awhile for the night sky to stop its dizzying spin about his head. When it had he pulled the pinto about and rode back toward the timber.

Four days later Fargo awoke, not quite sure what day it was. It was cold. He was certain of that much. Squinting up at the sun, Fargo saw it was no brighter than the moon. And it gave off precious little warmth. Overnight the mountains seemed to have lifted themselves into a colder, harsher climate.

His teeth chattering, he leaned his head back against his saddle. His throat was dry, his lips were cracked painfully, and there was no doubt he had a raging fever. As he reached up to his face to wipe away the cold sweat, he was surprised at how raw it felt to his touch. Exploring further, he noticed for the first time that the cabin fire had singed his eyebrows considerably.

But all that was nothing compared to the devouring pain in his side. Quinlan's blade had violated something deep and vital. Examining his wound a couple of days ago, Fargo had found maggots swarming in it. Indian medicine men had long been known to keep deep knife wounds clean by allowing maggots to feed on the putrefying flesh. And during his inspection of the wound, he had noticed that it did indeed appear somewhat fresher and cleaner. Nevertheless, he had clawed the maggots from it.

It was a fool thing to do, he now realized. And he was ashamed at his fastidiousness. He should have let the maggots do their work.

Pine Bluff was perhaps four more days away from his present position. He did not expect a warm welcome from Ike Landusky and his pals when he got there, but that could not be helped. He had no place else to go. Even so, there was no longer any certainty that he would make it back to Pine Bluff—or even that he was going in the right direction.

This observation shook Fargo out of his lethargy. He did not want to die. And certainly not at the hands of a dead man, for that was what Quinlan had been when he thrust up that knife of his. With deliberate care, Fargo laid bare his wound, then reached into his saddlebag for the bottle of bourbon. Unstoppering it, he rubbed the fiery liquid into his wound. The alcohol dug into the wound like a thousand tiny knives. Fargo almost groaned aloud. Instead, he laughed, stoppered the bottle, and returned it to his saddlebag.

His side blazing like a grass fire, he stood up and proceeded to break camp. It took almost an hour, but he persevered doggedly. By the time he was able to pull himself up into his saddle and ride off, he was riding into the teeth of a fierce, snow-laden wind.

The snow was a fine, hard grain that stung his eyes and soon cut his blistered face raw. He tied his hat on with his bandanna and donned his slicker, but the slicker soon became a stiff, almost unyielding mantle, offering minimal protection from the demented wind that now tore at him and the pinto.

Soon the trail ahead of him was white and the

trees bordering it only ghostly presences dimly visible through the swirling snow. Whenever a clump of trees was close enough to the trail to offer him shelter, he would pull in close to them to catch his breath for a while and let the pinto lick at the snow for moisture. But these opportunities were rare, and night found him camped in a rough lean-to with a howling wind at his back and a campfire that gave off only a promise of warmth. His fever was now a raging inferno within him, and he slept only fitfully.

When morning came, the wind had risen to maniacal fury and Fargo realized that in his condition there was no sense trying to make any more headway. And since the wind had shifted overnight, his present campsite offered little protection from the shrieking winds. Peering up at the slope behind him, he studied the steep, wooded flanks until he spotted a cluster of caves just above the treeline. He caught sight of them only occasionally through the shifting, eddying clouds of snow. They appeared as great hollowed eyes, staring blindly out from under beetling cliffs.

Fargo broke camp, then pulled the pinto after him through the mounting drifts as he struggled up through the timber. He lost track of time, but at last he reached the largest of two caves. Another, smaller cave was just below it, but Fargo chose the larger one so he could stable the pinto out of the storm's blast.

Stomping into the cave entrance, he kept going until he was far enough inside to escape the wind's blast. The ceiling of the cavern was at least thirty feet high. Peering back out through the entrance, he glimpsed, through the shifting curtains of snow, a high meadow off to his right. As soon as the snow let up, he could let the pinto graze there.

He turned then and went deeper into the cavern, and for the rest of that day, he occupied himself with building and keeping a fire. Before he crawled into his soogan that night, he took out the bourbon and again poured it liberally into his wound. The pain was excruciating, but he held the bottle steady as he poked the bottle's snout into the ragged, puckered hole left by Quinlan's knife. That accomplished, he fell back into an exhausted sleep, his body coiled about the fire.

The next morning Fargo awoke as weak as a kitten. It was the silence that had awakened him. Sitting up in his soogan, he found himself looking out over a bright white wasteland of snow. He got to his feet and walked to the mouth of the cavern, squinting to protect his eyes from the sunlight's dazzling reflection. Pleased though he was that this sudden, early storm had passed, he realized its ending had perhaps come too late for him. He could barely keep on his feet.

It occurred to him then what was wrong. In addition to his loss of blood, he had not eaten in days.

He was about to turn back to build a new fire when out onto the meadow to his right raced a young grizzly, a young badger in its jaws. Behind came four big wolves, a female and her mate and two almost full-grown cubs. Overtaken in the middle of the immaculate tablecloth of snow, the exasperated grizzly turned on the nearest wolf—the youngest of the four—and with a single powerful cuff sent the animal tumbling backward into a drift. But this stand only caused the grizzly to sink deeper into the snow. His progress slowed considerably, the older wolves, backs arched, fangs clicking, closed in on him like gray lightning bolts.

The young grizzly had the badger still in its mouth. With perfect teamwork, the two wolves passed on either side—the large male a second or two ahead of the female. The male's jaw closed over the badger's tail, yanking the badger out of the bear's mouth. Before the bear could go after him, the female snapped savagely at the bear's hind quarter, drawing him away from her mate.

Another wolf bowled into him, tumbling the young grizzly back into the deep snow, its four feet in the air. At once the youngest wolf flashed forward to rip and tear at the bear's exposed belly. Exploding with sudden rage and fear, the grizzly rose to its full height, uttering an anguished roar that shook the mountain. Turning swiftly, it slashed the air. One swipe caught one of the younger wolves and sent it tumbling back, yelping in shock and pain. A second later, it struggled to its feet and slunk off, a livid trail following him through the snow. Fargo could see how the wolf's back had been laid open from shoulder to ham.

But this only seemed to arouse the remaining wolves to greater fury. They darted in, struck at the bear, flashed away, spun about and struck from another direction. So swiftly did they move and so effective were their powerful, snapping jaws that the bear appeared to be losing ground. The young grizzly was no longer fighting to keep the badger. It was fighting for its life

Absorbed in the battle, Fargo became aware only at the last minute that something vast and powerful was moving out from the smaller cave below him. Looking down, he saw the hump of a full-grown grizzly. Obviously it had just settled into its winter bed and was more than a little disturbed by this unseemly tumult outside its den. Anxious to punish those responsible, it dropped to all fours and with a series of deep, surly grunts, plowed through the snow toward the battle in the clearing.

With awesome power, the grizzly lay about with its long, fearsome claws. The scalp of the male wolf was peeled back. A second later the other young wolf limped off, yelping piteously, dragging the shattered, bloody stump of its hind leg.

The battle was over that quickly.

Even so, as the mother wolf flashed off after her torn and dismembered family, she snatched the remains of the badger out of the snow and took it with her.

Both grizzlies now rose on their hind legs and stared at each other, the older towering over the younger one. Not a sound was uttered by either animal. But after a second or two, the younger one came down soundlessly in the snow, turned swiftly, and shambled back across the field to disappear down the slope. The big one dropped back onto its four feet then and plowed back through the snow to its cave.

As he did so, Fargo ducked back into the cavern out of sight. But he was not fast enough. The grizzly caught a glimpse of him and halted. For a moment it tipped its head slightly, studying Fargo. Then, almost with a visible shrug of its massive shoulders, it continued on into its own cave.

It was then that Fargo caught sight of the sprawled carcass staining the pristine meadowland before him. It was that of the youngest wolf. At once Fargo felt the saliva gathering in his mouth. His jaw ached. Grabbing his knife, he donned his slicker and started from the cavern.

But in his sudden eagerness, he forgot his wound. The pain that sliced up his side when he took his first quick stride caused him to double over, then sprawl headlong, his head spinning. Cursing, he pushed himself upright, shaking his head in chagrin. Hell! There was no hurry, he told himself. That wolf wasn't going anywhere. Carefully, gritting his teeth from the pain, he pushed himself upright and limped out of the cavern.

By the time he reached the wolf, it was cold but not yet stiff, the body stretched out as far as it could go. Even in death it seemed to be fleeing the grizzly's terrible claws. Straddling the still form, Fargo rolled the wolf over onto its back. Then he plunged his bowie deep into the animal's chest and ripped it down the length of the carcass to the crotch. Reaching into the steaming vitals, he pulled forth the animal's liver, sliced it quickly, and devoured it raw.

Almost at once he felt a lift.

Then he took the wolf by the tail, slung it over his shoulder, and lugged it back to the cave. Once there, he rebuilt his fire, skinned the animal, and cooked the haunches. It was not long before he was feasting on wolf meat, and by midafternoon he was busy jerking over his campfire the little meat that remained.

As Fargo worked, a gray veil of clouds slipped across the sky, blotting out the sun. And with the clouds came a sudden, icy breath of wind. By sundown, there was snow again—this time with a silent, awesome density that appalled Fargo. It was as if someone were standing over the cavern entrance emptying an enormous pillowcase.

Nevertheless, Fargo felt much better. After swabbing out his wound with generous portions of bourbon, he allowed himself the luxury of a few hefty belts from the bottle before coiling up around his campfire. The last thing he remembered before dropping off was the gentle, comforting nicker of his pinto back in the cavern.

Two days later, the second storm showing no sign of letting up, Fargo realized he had to make a run for the valley. He had used up the remainder of the wolf meat and he was getting weak again.

The first day, he made good-enough time, allowing the pinto to rest up frequently and never pushing him too hard. He camped along a stream bank, in a snug arbor he found under a dense tangle of berry vines and mountain laurel. The snow had drifted over it, forming a solid roof. Fargo cut several evergreen boughs and piled them on the ground inside the arbor. Then he lit a fire just outside the entrance and ate what remained of his jerky. His belly full, he crawled in under his roof of snow and lay down on the evergreen boughs. His pinto he had left in the pines above the river. The thought of wolves crossed his mind, and he said a silent prayer for the pinto's safety before dropping off into an exhausted sleep.

When he awoke, he found himself in pitch darkness. For an instant he panicked—until he realized what had happened. Thrusting himself out through the entrance, he used his head and shoulders to break a way through the wall of solid snow. Once in the clear, he looked around. It was still snowing, and during the night the wind had shifted to the northeast, sifting a huge drift over the arbor. As Fargo struggled through the waist-high drifts on his way up into the pines to see to the pinto, he almost wished he were back in his snug cave, so cruel were the snow-laden winds that now slashed and howled at him.

He was not able to get under way until what he assumed was close to midday, and when a gloomy, howling night descended on him once again, he was almost too weak to take care of the pinto and fashion himself a shelter for the night. How far he had gone this day, he had no idea, and he was finding it difficult to shake a heavy sense of foreboding. His wound was on fire once again and his raging fever had returned with a vengeance.

On the third day after leaving the cave, having no clear idea just how far he had traveled, Fargo camped in among a small stand of pines, under a clumsily constructed lean-to. Overhead, the snow swirled blindingly with no hint of moon or stars. The wind screeched through the pines with an intensity that set his chattering teeth on edge. He inspected his wound by the light of his dim fire and found it—incredibly—alive with maggots again. With clumsy, half-frozen fingers, he tried to wipe them from the wound, but gave it up at last and coiled himself about the fire, the bottle of bourbon in his hands. He drank his fill, emptying the bottle, then drew as close to the fire as he could get without setting fire to his bedroll, and slept.

His sleep was disordered, fevered, and he awoke in a panic, shivering violently. The fire had gone out. It was only a black socket in the snow. Above the pines, the blizzard still howled in full fury. He sat up weakly, aware of the maggots crawling in his wound, but aware also that he no longer cared. He was enormously tired. His eyelids were leaden. The snow had driven in through the lean-to and covered his soogan. He let his head sink back down and let the insane fury of the wind lull him.

He was in no hurry, he told himself. There was no one waiting for him in Pine Bluff, except a man who might want to murder him. Why not rest awhile and let this damn blizzard blow itself out? It couldn't last forever.

He coiled into a ball, closed his eyes, and waited for the numbing tide of sleep to bear him away from this awesome, vindictive cold. But the persistent ache in his side would not let him sleep, nor would the constant, unremitting chatter of his teeth or the violent shudders that occasionally racked him. At last he raised his head. His body was simply refusing to betray him—even if his will to survive *had* abandoned him.

He struggled out of his bedroll. Like a drunken man, he fell often. But he paid it no heed and managed somehow to pack his bedroll and the rest of his gear, find the pinto, and mount up. As he rode off through the shrieking, white universe, he allowed the pinto's good sense to guide him.

He rode all that day, a white rag doll clinging to the horse, too weak to think of dismounting. This time, he realized, if he got off the pinto, he would never get back on again. Despite the incredible cold, he was on fire. His left side was encased in a chilling armor of frozen blood that had begun oozing from his wound earlier when he broke camp.

Night was falling. He was dimly aware that the pinto was no longer moving cautiously downhill. It was crossing a level stretch. A particularly vicious gust of wind caught his frozen slicker and almost pulled him off the pinto. The sudden, erratic shift in his weight caused the pinto to stumble, then stop, his head down. Fargo took a deep breath and urged the pony gently forward. With what felt like an enormous, trembling sigh the pinto started up again.

Abruptly a black, sparkling window appeared in the clouds of snow that swirled about him. Stars, brilliant and winking, and a moon—as serene and untroubled as a woman's face—gazed down upon him. The ragged window in the windswept cloud shifted. This time Fargo glimpsed the towering pine bluff that rose above the town. A second later, as swiftly as the window had opened, it closed, and the stinging, wind-driven snow tore at his face once again.

But that one glimpse had been enough. The pine bluff's location told him he was south of the town. If he were to keep on his present course, he would miss it completely.

Slowly, carefully, he turned the exhausted pinto. As he rode now, the lacerating wind whipped at his left side with renewed fury. He realized then that he had been letting the storm drive him south in order to protect his wound. The wind had shifted again and this time it was a blue norther he was fighting.

And it had almost beaten him.

The hotel was the most visible building in the town as he rode slowly down the main street. No other riders were abroad. The sidewalks were piled high with drifts. He saw only a few lights in the windows. Riding around to the rear of the hotel, he slipped wearily off the pinto and approached the livery doors. They were closed as tightly as a miser's fist. For an infuriating moment Fargo stood before it, his head rocking, his body trembling. Had he ridden all this way to freeze to death in front of a stable's locked doors?

He remounted carefully, deliberately, and rode back out of the alley and around to the front of the hotel. With numbed fingers, he tied the pinto to the hitch rail, then stumbled up the porch steps and lurched toward the door. At least three feet of snow had drifted against it. He lowered his shoulder, pushed against the door with his full weight, and burst into the hotel's lobby.

The heat inside the place smote him like a fist from the bowels of hell. Fargo felt the skin on his face shrivel. He staggered toward the desk and found himself looking into Ronald Burton's astonished face.

"My God, sir," cried the man.

"My horse," Fargo managed, his mouth working clumsily. "He's out there. Take care of him."

Burton was already out from behind the desk. "Of course, sir," he told him. "Of course!"

Fargo saw Betty then. She was hurrying from the dining room, eyes wide. He took a step away from the front desk and felt her hands on his shoulder as she guided him toward the staircase. Reaching the foot of the stairs, he looked up the long flight and knew he would never be able to make it.

He lost his balance. The stairs rushed up at him. He heard Betty scream as he plunged forward through the stairs and into darkness . . .

6

Almost a week after the second norther hit, the snow cover, though it had melted considerably, was giving Jed Two Shoes trouble. His old eyes had difficulty with the glare. But this did little to dampen his spirits. He had just returned from laying more traps, and after being cooped up in his cabin, he was pleased to be out and active once again. Besides, his cabin had begun to stink.

Standing by a large flat rock in front of his cabin, he was working over his second beaver pelt of the day. The pelt was stretched out flat on top of the rock, fur side down, and Jed was scraping off every last particle of flesh and fat with his knife and a stone chisel.

A small earthenware bowl was sitting in the snow beside him. Into this he dropped the fat and flesh. Later, he would boil these scrapings into a thick, gelatinous soup. He had already removed the beaver's brains and set them aside to give the soup body.

Jed worked intently, enjoying the clear cold air and the smell of the freshly fallen snow. The first storm of the year always pleased him. This one had been a real bleeder, but he took it for what it was, a good-natured warning. For that was all it was, a harbinger of what was yet to come when winter really set in. The snowfalls he considered genuine—the god-awful, 150-percent blizzards—were those that lasted a fortnight at least. By his reckoning, these were a good two months away yet.

Still, this one had been a fine beginning, especially so early in the season. It sure as hell had put the grizzlies on the alert. They were growing frantic in their efforts to pile on the tallow for their long winter sleep. Whenever Jed came upon them, they were miserable and short-tempered. So far, Jed was lucky. He had not yet come upon Old Silver Hump.

Jed chuckled to himself as he worked over the pelt. The Nez Percé insisted the grizzlies were real people—a race apart. They were certain bears could think and understand like humans. Jed didn't think he wanted to believe that. People were bad enough for neighbors, but bears that acted and thought like people? No, sir. He had enough to contend with as it was.

Still, the more he saw of Old Silver Hump and the rest of the grizzlies in this valley, the more difficult it became for him to discount what the Nez Percé believed so strongly. In his prime now and close to nine hundred pounds, Old Silver Hump acted like a proper Indian chief, cuffing his women around and lording it over every other grizzly in the valley. His claw marks on the trees were the tallest by far, and it was his trails that were the deepest and most thoroughly worn.

Jed gave him as wide a berth as possible. Even so, he was certain the bear knew all about him and was tolerating his presence in this valley only grudgingly. Perhaps, Jed mused as he scraped away on his beaver pelt, he should go find Old Silver Hump when he woke up next spring and offer to smoke the peace pipe with him.

If the bear took the pipe and began smoking it, that would prove the Nez Percé were right—and Jed would clear out.

Chuckling at his joke, Jed glanced up.

Startled, he almost dropped his stone chisel. A woman was riding out of the pines behind his cabin. She was pulling a pack horse behind her. She looked incredibly haggard, with long, stringy hair and hollow cheeks. As she rode closer toward him, he saw that her eyes seemed to have sunken almost out of sight in their sockets.

And yet, there was something oddly young, almost girlish, about this mounted apparition.

Hastily putting down the chisel and sheathing his knife, Jed started across the snow to meet her. She pulled up as he approached. He kept going until he was a few feet in front of her. Then he halted in his tracks. He had seen a madman once, and it had sent an icy terror coursing through his vitals.

This time he was looking at a madwoman.

The woman's eyes shifted from him . . . to someone approaching Jed from behind. He swung around, his

101

right hand dropping to his knife. He was too late as the barrel of a six-gun slammed him on the forehead. A bright light shattered the universe. He was flung backward into the snow, his head roaring fiercely. As Jed blinked up at the giant towering over him, a bright-red curtain flowed down over his eyes.

He wiped the blood from his eyes and slowly, groggily regained his feet.

The son of a bitch who had struck him was better than six feet. His lean face was covered with a red stubble, and sticking out from under his wide-brimmed hat was an unruly shock of flaming red hair. His shoulders were massive, and thick, knotted muscles bulged under his heavy deerskin jacket. A blood-soaked bandage was wound tightly around his right thigh.

"That ain't very friendly," Jed growled, "comin' up behind a body and sluggin' him like that. What you have to do that for, mister?"

The man smiled. That is, his mouth twisted upward slightly. There was no change in the mean, feverish light in his eyes. "Didn't know what kind of a welcome I'd get," he drawled.

"My cabin's back there," Jed told the man, dimly aware of the woman still on her horse behind him. "Take what you need and leave me alone."

"It's you who's goin' to leave."

Jed frowned. "What's that?"

"You heard me."

"This here's my valley. That's my cabin. I ain't leavin' here."

The big redhead thumb-cocked his weapon. "One way or another you're goin' to leave here, old man. I found this valley four years ago and been meanin' to come back all that time. Now I'm back, and I'm staying. But you're goin'."

The man lifted the revolver. The muzzle looked as wide as the mouth of a cannon to Jed. He swallowed and looked back at the redhead. "You mean you're tellin' me this here's your valley just because you came on it four years ago?"

"That's what I'm tellin' you."

Jed moistened his lips. His forehead was throbbing and seemed to be growing heavier with each passing second. Obviously, he was in no position to argue with this madman in front of him. But it tore his heart out to give up his valley without an argument.

"Hell, mister. You ain't even givin' me a chance to bargain."

"This here weapon's all the cards I need. You can argue with it if you want." He smiled. "Go ahead. Argue. I'll drop you where you stand. By spring the wolves and the coyotes will leave only your bones for me to scatter. Take your choice, old man."

Jed shook his head slowly, all fight draining out of him. "Let me get my gear out of my cabin," he said wearily.

The big man smiled, stepped back, and holstered his weapon.

"All right. But you go unarmed and on foot," he told Jed. "I can use those horses you got behind the cabin."

"You mean I can't take my rifle?"

"I need one."

Jed started to protest, then shrugged, turned, and

103

headed back to his cabin. As the woman moved her horse aside for him, he glanced up into her ravaged countenance and saw her lips moving rapidly, silently. She was having a conversation with her private devil.

An hour or so before nightfall that same day, after following behind Jed on horseback to the limits of the valley, the redhead pulled up. Jed halted and looked back. Without a wave the man was leaving Jed to slog on alone through the heavy snow. As the big rider crested a hill, he pulled up and looked back at Jed. As Jed watched him bitterly, he hefted the rifle he had taken from Jed, then vanished beyond the hill.

Jed was going over in his mind the possibility of doubling back that night and killing the big son of a bitch while he slept. But the odds were against him accomplishing anything. He'd get his head blown off. The only weapon he had left was his hunting knife. Jed turned back around, hefted his back pack higher onto his shoulders, and kept going toward the far pass.

A week later, Harry Carson, a bullwhacker hastening his mule team through the snow with well-seasoned epithets, pulled back suddenly on his reins and brought his team to a walk.

A bent, yet sturdy old man had appeared out of a snow bank beside the trail just ahead of him. He had a clean, snowy beard, sharp blue eyes, and rosy cheeks. His wide floppy hat had seen better days, as had his near-ruined sheepskin jacket. As Carson got closer to the man, he noticed a long, discolored welt running the length of the man's forehead.

He pulled his team to a halt alongside the stranger and switched his chaw to the other cheek.

"You waitin' for spring?" he asked.

"Nope. Waitin' for a ride," the old fellow replied. "Which way you headin'?"

"South."

"Ain't nothin' much in that direction. I was hopin' you'd be goin' toward Fort Billin's."

"Nope. Pine Bluff. Got a load of real fancy furniture for a hotel there. Come around the Horn, it did—all the way from England. You want a ride?"

"Might as well," the old man said, clambering up beside Carson.

"I don't suppose you'd be wantin' to tell me what in hell you'd be doin' out here in the middle of a snow bank—with no firepower and a storm comin' on?"

"That's right, friend," the old man replied. "I sure as hell wouldn't. It would be too embarrassin'. Much obliged for the lift, though."

The bullwhacker nodded. He wasn't goin to press the matter. He was too glad for the company. Sending a dark plume of tobacco juice into a white snowdrift, he picked up his bullwhip and sent it crackling over the backs of his mules.

Fargo shrugged out of his sheepskin jacket and tossed it onto the bed, then looked out the window at Pine Bluff's dark buildings and empty streets. Except for the saloon, there was no hint of activity. Though there was a lamp on the table beside him, he did not light it. He had been holed up in this hotel now for better than two weeks, and as far as he knew, Ike Landusky was still unaware of his presence in Pine Bluff. For now, he wanted to keep it that way.

The door opened softly behind him, then closed. Fargo recognized Betty's soft footsteps and turned as she approached him. In the darkened room he could just make out the pale oval of her face.

"Did you go far?" she asked, walking on past him and pulling down the window shade.

"Just to the foot of the bluff and back," he told her. "There wasn't much snow left. It felt good to stretch my legs."

"I'll bet it did." She lit the lamp on the dresser. "How does your side feel?"

"Almost as good as new."

"That's hard to believe, Skye. My father says you must have the constitution of a horse."

"Just so long as I don't have the face of one," Fargo replied. "I was in pretty bad shape, huh?"

She frowned, recalling his condition. "First of all, there were those burns on your face and hands, and the frostbite, and that ugly knife wound in your side. My God, Skye, I can still see those maggots crawling in it. I shudder every time I think of it."

"I know. I think I remember you washing them out. You used hot soapy water. *Very* hot soapy water." He grinned suddenly. "But I'm not complaining, believe me. By the way, what was that commotion I heard downstairs today?"

"Would you believe it?" she replied. "We finally got our shipment from England. The rest of our restaurant and lobby furniture. It came all the way around the Horn."

"Remarkable."

"It came the day before and we spent yesterday putting down the rugs and bringing in the new furniture. You won't recognize the lobby and the restaurant."

He smiled. "I'm looking forward to seeing it."

"And something else. With the furniture we got an old mountain man!"

"A what?"

She laughed. "You heard me. The teamster picked him up in the mountains north of here. He helped us move in the furniture and now he's offered to work in the livery for his room and board this winter. Of course Dad's delighted. And so am I. Now I can concentrate on the restaurant."

The pleased excitement in Betty's voice as she related this good news to Fargo warmed him. He found himself closing his arms about her, wondering as he did why in hell he had waited so long. Enclosing her in his arms seemed as natural—and as inevitable—as breathing. She turned her head and rested it on his powerful chest.

"I was beginning to wonder-" she said with a sigh, "If you were *ever* going to do that."

He chuckled and held her closer. "It's not been easy keeping myself from it, and that's a fact."

"Why on earth *should* you keep yourself from doing it?" she demanded. "It's all I have wanted since you returned."

"Until now," he said, "I just haven't felt up to it.

But that walk seems to have done it for me." He chuckled. "I think I am going to live."

He lifted her chin and kissed her full on the lips. He had expected a chaste response. What he got instead was an embrace so fiery that he felt his head spin. Lifting Betty in his arms, he carried her over to his bed, put her down gently, and began to undress her.

She let him, for a while. But his fumbling fingers made her impatient. With a soft giggle, she pushed his hands away and finished undressing herself. Then she reached out and began to unbuckle his belt. He kicked off his boots, and in a minute her adept hands had skinned him. He eased onto the bed beside her and kissed her again. As her ravenous mouth opened to his probing lips, she reached her hand down and grabbed his throbbing erection.

"Oh, God," she breathed at the feel of him. Then she squeezed.

He slipped his tongue in deeper. She gave a tiny shudder. Her tongue met his. He felt the warm sweetness of it. The sweet scent of her breath was intoxicating. For a moment he could not get enough of her lips, and then with a gasp, she pulled back, eased her body higher on the bed, and thrust her breasts toward his face. He had not realized until that moment how large they were—and how saucily they were curved, with sharp, eagerly thrusting, rosy tips.

His mouth closed about one of them. She gasped with delight and squeezed his erection so tightly, that he was afraid she might break it off. But he paid no heed as his tongue caressed her nipple, every now and then flicking over the hard, thrusting tip. She cried out with pleasure each time he did this. Moaning softly, she tore the nipple from his mouth and thrust her other breast toward him, grinding against him frantically, her free hand pressing his head down upon her full, snowy breast.

By this time, his need for her—and her need for him—was beginning to take over. Reaching back, he covered them both with the bedspread. At once the heat of their bodies increased tenfold. Sweat stood out on his forehead. Tiny tiny beads of perspiration formed on her face as he sucked on her breasts. Her eyes became wanton slits. She pressed eagerly, hungrily against him, her hands still closed about his erection, as if she were unwilling to let it go for fear she would lose it forever.

He lifted his mouth from her breasts and looked down at her. She understood and rolled over onto her back and spread her legs eagerly. He glanced down at her body. Her pale flesh glowed under their canopy. She was narrow-hipped, with a flat stomach and a dark triangle already gleaming with moisture. He placed his big hand gently down upon her muff, then clasped her pubic mound and squeezed.

Her breath drew in with a long gasp. She thrust her buttocks off the bed, lunging upward fiercely. He freed her hand from his erection, bent his head, and kissed her flat stomach, his lips brushing down almost to her pubis.

"Ooooh! Oh, God!" Betty murmured.

She took his head with both hands and crushed his lips down upon her throbbing pubis. As she began to undulate wildly, Fargo ran his tongue gently over her tummy, up through her cleft, then kissed her on the mouth hard, his tongue meeting hers in a furious, wanton embrace.

At the same time he eased over onto her. He was barely aware of his erection passing into her until the searing moisture of her muff closed about him like a fist and drew him deep, deep within her. It was as if she still had him by the hand.

She sighed. "Yes, Skye! Yes! That's it. But deeper, please! Go deeper!"

He pressed into her, probing urgently. Her breath came in sharp, short bursts. Strange, inarticulate sounds broke from deep in her throat as she flung her arms around his back, pulling him still closer. Abruptly, her legs swung up, her ankles locking behind his back. Her hips began to gyrate furiously.

"Jesus, oh, oh, my God, Skye . . . Skye!"

Her mouth fought hungrily for his, her tongue quivering against his, arousing him to a frenzy. He plunged deeper and still deeper, impaling her with a wild, murderous abandon. Abruptly, her mouth tore away from his as her head arched backward. Ducking his head once more to her breasts, he enclosed a nipple with his mouth, nipping crazily at it with his teeth until it became as hard as a rock. This drove her wild. She began thrashing up at him with a fury that almost sent him out of her. He clung to her, bore her down relentlessly beneath him, meeting each of her thrusts with one of his own.

Soon, all deliberation, all design, left him. He was past the point of no return, pounding her so hard he was only dimly aware of the thrashing woman beneath him. He was leaning over her, riding her full out, breaking through the timber at last. A laugh broke from him exultantly as his head snapped back in the sheer, pure joy of it. He began pulsing within her, exploding. She gasped, thrusting up toward him with each throbbing expulsion.

"My God, Skye!" she muttered furiously. "Don't stop!"

Laughing, he started thrusting again as her fists pounded on his back. Abruptly, her hips leapt upward. She uttered a deep, moaning wail as her explosion came—an intense, deep shuddering that shook her from crown to toe.

Afterward, she clung to him, still quivering, holding him to her, flesh locked into flesh, until at last she fell away from him, uttering a long, deep sigh.

Reaching out, she brushed a wet lock of his hair off his forehead, her eyes filled with pure wonder. "That was good," she said.

"Yes." He dropped beside her, rolled over onto his back, and pulled her head and shoulders up onto his chest.

She draped an arm over his waist and kissed the heavy coil of hair that matted his chest. Then she draped one silken limb over his legs.

For a long while they said nothing. Then she spoke softly. "You're much better."

He chuckled. "Yes."

"Does that mean you'll be leaving soon?"

"I suppose so."

"Red Ericson?"

"Yes."

"But you don't even know where he is."

"He's somewhere in the mountains north of here.

I'll find him. He'll have to hole up, now that winter's set in."

"Yes, I suppose so."

"By the way, I've been meaning to ask you. When I rode out before, was that gunfire I heard?"

"Yes, she replied. "Ike's men charged the hotel. Dad fired his shotgun over their heads to warn them off. But it didn't stop them. Thank God you were gone by that time."

"Did Landusky give your dad any trouble when he found I was gone?"

"No." She smiled ironically. "If Ike and his men want a good meal from time to time—or a decent place to bunk—they have to rely on us. And Ike knew Dad was in his rights. He warned them they were trespassing."

"Your old man has balls."

"Yes," she admitted, hugging him. "He has. And so have you." She nipped at the hair on his chest.

"Tomorrow morning," he said, "I think I'll come down for breakfast."

She didn't say anything for a minute, realizing what this meant. When the other townsmen who breakfasted in the hotel saw Fargo, they would waste no time informing Ike Landusky.

"All right," she said finally, making the best of it. "When you come down, you can see how nice those new furnishings look in the lobby and in the restaurant."

Her hand moved slyly down his stomach to his crotch.

"My!" she cried. "Just look at this!"

"You look."

"I don't need to. I can *feel* it."

"What do you think we should do about it?"

"I'll show you," she said.

She swung her leg all the way over his waist, mounted him, and with reckless speed, grabbed his massive erection and sat back down on him. Hard. His engorged rod lunged swiftly past her labia as she sucked it so deep inside her that he was certain he had struck bottom. Sighing deeply, she flung her head back, then began rocking rhythmically back and forth.

Fargo closed his eyes, moving contentedly in time with her, his big hands reaching up to fondle her nipples. They were not gentle and he heard her suck in her breath with delight. This time he hoped it would take longer than the last—and that she would stay with him through the night.

7

As soon as Betty slipped from his room the next morning, Fargo gave himself a leisurely whore's bath with whiskey and water, shaved, and dressed. Then he clapped on his hat and left the room.

When he reached the lobby, he found a remarkably fresh, bright-eyed Betty standing in the restaurant doorway, apparently waiting for him. With an impish smile, she told him how surprised and pleased she was to see that he was well enough to come down for breakfast.

Her father, at work behind the front desk, glanced up and seemed equally pleased that Fargo was well enough to come down for breakfast. "Good morning, Mr. Fargo," he said. "It's good to see you on your feet once again."

"Thank you," Fargo replied. "Betty's been telling me about the new furniture, so I thought I'd come down and see for myself."

"Delighted, Mr. Fargo. Delighted."

As Fargo glanced about the small lobby, he noted a large grandfather clock ticking solidly away in the corner, already sounding like an old friend. And on the floor under his feet a new, thick, richly patterned rug had been put down.

He smiled at Betty. "Very nice," he said.

"Yes, Dad and I are very pleased," she told him, taking his arm and leading him into the dining room. "Now come along. I want you to meet Jed Two Shoes."

Betty led him to the large table near a window at the back of the restaurant. Already seated and waiting for his breakfast was an old man with a full beard and a thick mane of snow-white hair that swept back off his impressive brow all the way to his square, solid shoulders. It was obvious from the set of his jaw and the fullness of his mouth that he still had all his teeth. His cheeks were pink, and his eyes—as alive and bright as those of a young man—were almost as blue as Fargo's. Indeed, despite the fact that he must have been in his seventies, there was an alertness about the way he looked up as Fargo approached that argued for a man considerably younger.

Betty introduced them and Fargo found the mountain man's grip as powerful as his own. Fargo sat down, and after taking his order, Betty left. Peering more closely at Jed Two Shoes' face, Fargo saw the faint trace of a recent laceration that ran almost the length of his forehead.

"That your pinto I been admirin'?" Jed asked, smiling.

"The Ovaro?"

"Yep. That's the one. Nice piece of horseflesh."

Fargo nodded. "That pinto has taken me through hell and back. Give it a little extra, will you, Jed?"

"Been doin' that already."

"Thanks."

"He'll be a mite rambunctious when you take him out. He's real fat and sassy now. But all he needs is a good run."

"That's just what I'll be giving him before long."

"You movin' out?"

"Soon's I finish my business here."

Jed Two Shoes nodded. The mountain man had enough sense not to ask what that business might be.

Their breakfasts arrived and the two men set to work in agreeable silence. When they had finished and were washing the food down with black coffee, Fargo glanced about him at the newly renovated dining room.

It was remarkable, the change the new furnishings had wrought. Hanging at the windows were drapes of a deep-maroon fabric brocaded with a bright-gold design. They might have seemed too heavy for the room, but the way Betty had hung them, they appeared just right. The morning sunlight brought out their rich wine color and brightened the room wondrously. A richly patterned rug covered the floor, absorbing every sound, muffling every footstep. The mahogany tables and chairs gleamed darkly.

At that moment Burt Physer and another man entered the restaurant and found a table across the room. Before Physer sat down, he glanced casually

116

in Fargo's direction. His mouth dropped open. Fargo waved to him. The startled barber sat down, then immediately leaned across the table to tell his friend who Fargo was. Fargo saw Physer's breakfast companion glance quickly in his direction.

Fargo looked away. The cat was out of the bag. Fargo was no longer a well-cared-for prisoner inside the St. James Hotel.

From his window, Fargo watched Burt Physer and his friend hurry along the muddy sidewalk toward the saloon. As soon as Physer disappeared inside, Fargo walked over to the corner by his bed and picked up his Sharps. He dropped a cartridge into the magazine, then levered up the trigger guard. Shrugging into his sheepskin coat, he left the room.

When he reached the lobby, Betty was waiting for him. Beside her stood her father. Both noticed the rifle in his hand.

"What are you going to do?" Burton asked Fargo.

"I understand the last time I rode out of here, you had some trouble. I don't want that to happen next time I leave."

"But, my dear sir, how can you possibly handle that gang of desperadoes by yourself?"

Fargo smiled. "Let me worry about that."

Betty spoke up. "I wish you wouldn't go out there, Skye."

"I don't see I have any choice in the matter, Betty. I can't stay holed up in this hotel forever."

Betty compressed her lips and said nothing more.

Pushing open the door, Fargo strode out onto the porch and paused to get his bearings. For a moment he was blinded by the glare of the bright morning sunlight on the snow still on the ground. Muddy ruts ran like dirty slashes down the center of the street. Beyond the town, the snow cover on the bluff gleamed in the bright sunlight. Fargo took a deep breath. It felt good to be out at last. Out in the open.

He stepped off the porch and started down the street toward the saloon. From behind him came the clump of heavy footsteps on the hotel porch. Fargo pulled up and turned around. Burton and Jed Two Shoes were striding across the porch. Burton was carrying his double-barrel shotgun, and Jed Two Shoes had stuck an enormous revolver into his belt. The weapon looked like a Walker Colt. A very concerned Betty was peering out the door after them.

"What in blazes you doin' with that cannon?" Fargo asked Jed.

"Just bought it from Mr. Burton."

Fargo looked at the hotel owner. "I wish you'd stay out of this, Burton. It's my fight, not yours. You and Betty will have to live in this town long after I'm gone."

Jed Two shoes turned to Burton. "Fargo's right, Mr. Burton. Think of that girl of yours. No sense in gettin' your head shot off. Fargo and me, we can handle this."

Burton hesitated.

"This is not your fight, Burton," Fargo told him patiently.

The hotel owner took a deep, troubled breath, then turned and went back inside, pulling Betty in after him.

Fargo peered at Jed. "You sure you want to be a

118

part of this, Jed? Like I told Burton. This here's my fight."

The mountain man stepped off the porch and came to a halt beside Fargo. "I'll tell you how it is, Fargo," he said. "Not too long ago, this son had to swaller a ton of shit without bein' able to scratch back. You might say this here's my way of fixin' the hurt in my pride." Jed Two Shoes started down the street. "Now, what do you say we stop all this palaver and get on down there?"

With a sudden smile, Fargo fell in beside the mountain man.

Landusky had posted a man outside the saloon to watch for him. As soon as he saw Fargo and Jed Two Shoes approaching, he ducked back inside. At once the Indian bar girls and half a dozen patrons streamed out of the saloon, Burt Physer and the saloon's owner in the lead. A moment later, Ike Landusky and two others strode from the saloon, then fanned out across the street.

Fargo held up. Jed lifted the Walker Colt from his belt. Landusky took out his six-gun. His two sidekicks did the same.

"You've bought it, Fargo," Landusky called. "You ain't sneakin' out this time. But I don't hold no grudge for shootin' up my place. Throw down your weapon and maybe I'll go easy on you."

"Maybe?"

Landusky laughed. It was an unpleasant laugh. "You heard me."

"Spread out," Fargo told Jed. "Make for cover. We got more than those three over there to deal with, I'm thinking."

Jed nodded. "That's what I been figurin' too."

Fargo and Jed darted suddenly in opposite directions. At once Landusky and his two gunslicks brought up their guns and began blasting. As Fargo ducked into the alley beside the saloon, a swarm of slugs tore apart the weathered shingles on the corner. Fargo kept going until he reached the back alley that ran behind the saloon. Glancing back, he saw Jed Two Shoes across the street, crouching behind a barrel in front of the barbershop, his big Colt blazing.

Fargo ducked down the back alley. Ahead of him a head appeared from a doorway, then ducked back. Fargo flattened himself against the wall and waited. Abruptly, the gunman darted from cover, his gun blazing. As slugs slammed into the wall beside him, Fargo crouched, firing the Sharps from his hip. The slug punched into the gunman's belly, just above his belt buckle. The force of the slug flung the man clear across the alley. He struck the corner of a privy and slid to the ground.

Fargo reloaded and kept going.

He reached the saloon's rear porch and stepped up onto it. The back door was ajar. He poked it open with his rifle barrel. Fargo heard shots coming from the street in front of the saloon, and looking across the empty saloon out through the front window, he saw one of Landusky's men darting for cover. He never made it as Jed Two Shoes brought him down.

Crouching, Fargo eased himself into the saloon, keeping close to the wall. He heard a footfall behind him on the back porch. Darting behind the bar, he lifted his Sharps and waited. A shadow appeared in the doorway. The door was pushed open. A tall fellow, gun drawn, stepped into the saloon and glanced in Fargo's direction. Fargo saw the sudden, startled look on his face a split second before he pulled the Sharps' trigger. The slug slammed into the man's face, smashing it to a pulp and hurtling him back out through the door, his twitching gun hand firing into the ceiling.

Fargo ducked down behind the bar, reloaded, then hurried across the saloon floor to peer out over the top of the batwings. Jed Two Shoes had cleared the street. Directly across from the saloon two of Landusky's men had flattened themselves against an alley wall and were making only a feeble effort to return Jed's fire.

But where the hell was Landusky?

A creaking board on the rear porch alerted Fargo. He ducked away from the doorway just as a Colt blazed—followed by a fusillade. Slugs ripped through the batwings' flimsy slats, while others ricocheted off the top of the bar. Firing as they came, Ike Landusky and two of his men boiled into the saloon. Keeping low, Fargo charged up the stairs to the narrow balcony.

When he reached the top, he found himself staring at Brad Poucher. The prospector was standing by the balcony railing, waiting patiently for him, his right wrist wrapped in a filthy bandage.

In his left hand, he held an already cocked revolver.

"Hello, Fargo," Poucher said, squeezing the trigger.

But Fargo was already diving to the floor of the

balcony. As Poucher's round struck the wall behind him, Fargo swung up his Sharps and fired. A hole appeared in Poucher's dirty shirt front. The bullet's impact hurled the big prospector back through the balcony railing.

Fargo scrambled to his feet and raced down the balcony toward a window. He heard Landusky and the other two with him pounding up the stairs after him. Lowering his shoulder, he launched himself through the window, landing on the porch roof amid a shower of glass. Still clutching the Sharps, he leapt to the ground.

Reloading, Fargo flattened himself against the wall and waited. Someone eased himself through the broken glass and dropped to the roof above him. At the same time, from within the saloon, came the clatter of boots descending the stairs, then pounding toward him across the saloon. A second later a tall fellow in a floppy hat burst out the rear door onto the back porch. Fargo stepped away from the wall and fired point-blank, catching Ike's gunman high in the chest. As the impact of the bullet flung him back, he slammed into Landusky, who was just behind him. Landusky swore and fled back into the saloon.

Behind Fargo came a powerful detonation. He spun and saw Landusky's third gunman pitch forward off the porch roof. The fellow landed on his belly, his face in the mud. He did not move. Jed Two Shoes, his big Walker smoking, strode into view from around the corner of the building.

"Looks like that's the lot of 'em," he told Fargo.

"Not quite," Fargo said. "Landusky's still inside."

"I'll go around the other side," Jed said, and disappeared.

Fargo leaned his Sharps against the porch and took out his Colt. He needed more rapid fire now, he realized. Easing himself up onto the porch, he heard Landusky dragging tables and piling chairs. Keeping low, he sidled into the saloon. A shot from the other end of the saloon blew a hole in the wall inches above Fargo's head. Fargo ducked and blasted at the barricade of chairs and tables from behind which Landusky's shot had come, then ducked for cover behind the bar.

Landusky's head appeared suddenly behind a gun barrel. Fargo fired and ducked back. The slug smashed into the table in front of Landusky. Landusky fired twice in quick succession. Fargo kept his head down as the bar mirror behind him splintered and showered him with shards of glass.

Then he heard Jed Two Shoes on the front porch.

"I'm coming in, Fargo," he boomed.

"Keep down," Fargo called back. "Landusky's in the corner!"

Jed Two Shoes burst in. Fargo jumped up. Landusky's head and shoulders were visible as he turned to face Jed. Fargo fired his Colt—and kept on firing. The hail of slugs slammed Landusky back against the wall. For a second or two he clung to it like a monstrous, untidy fly. Then he slipped out of sight behind the barricade.

Fargo straightened, skirted the bar, and walked over to Landusky. Jed Two Shoes joined him.

"He's dead, sure enough," Jed said, sticking his

Walker Colt back into his belt. "You figure maybe now you could tell me what this was all about?"

Fargo turned and went back to get his Sharps. Jed accompanied him. Fargo picked up his Sharps, then started back to the hotel with Jed.

"Landusky has a stepbrother," Fargo told Jed, "and I want the son of a bitch's scalp. Ericson's his name. Red Ericson. But Landusky wasn't much help. He figured on stopping me."

"So now you'll be on your way—after this here Ericson feller."

"Yes," Fargo said.

"When?"

"As soon as I can saddle up." He glanced up at the sky. There were clouds, but there was no smell of snow in the air. "Before the next snow."

"Good luck."

"I'll need it."

An hour later, Fargo had laid out his supplies on his bedspread and was packing his gear when he heard a soft rap on his door. He walked over and opened it.

It was Betty. She entered, looking beyond Fargo at the bed. He closed the door behind her. She turned to him.

"You aren't wasting any time, Skye, are you?"

"You know how much I want Red Ericson, Betty."

"But can't you wait?"

"I told you, Betty. Ericson is in the mountains north of here. If this break in the weather continues, I still have a chance to track him. An oversized red-head with a half-crazy girl in tow should not be that

124

hard to track. That's Nez Percé country, and there's little that escapes them."

She started to argue, then evidently thought better of it. "All right," she sighed. "I knew I wouldn't have any luck trying to talk you out of it. But I just had to try. I'll miss you, Skye."

"And I'll miss you, Betty."

She walked into his arms. He kissed her. She answered his kiss passionately. After a moment she gently disengaged herself, turned, and left the room, closing the door firmly behind her.

Fargo stood for a moment, looking after her. Then he resumed packing his gear.

When Fargo rode out that afternoon, he headed north and kept going until late that night—when the Big Dipper was sitting alongside the North Star. Midnight. After selecting a site dry enough for his sleeping bag, he built a campfire, curled up close to it, and slept.

The aroma of hot coffee awoke him. He sat up. The campfire was blazing and a familiar figure was squatting beside it, sipping carefully at a steaming cup of coffee.

"What in blazes are you doing out here, Jed?" Fargo asked.

Jed Two Shoes was dressed in a low-crowned, floppy-brimmed hat and a newly acquired buffalo coat. The coat hung open and Fargo glimpsed the enormous Walker Colt stuck in his belt. A grin on his face, he handed Fargo a steaming cup of coffee.

"Yes, sir," he said, grinning. "There ain't nothin'

125

like the smell of hot coffee to shake a man out of his bunk."

"Never mind that, Jed," Fargo replied, taking the coffee and sipping it gratefully. "I want an explanation."

"Somethin' came up, but I'll tell you all about that soon's we get something under our belts."

Fargo shrugged, sipped a bit more of the scalding coffee, then reached first for his hat, then for his boots. While the Trailsman rolled up his bedding and saw to the rest of his morning toilet, Jed cooked the breakfast. The two men ate heartily. By the time camp was broken and the horses saddled, it was almost full light.

"Let's have it, Jed," Fargo said finally. "You promised me an explanation."

"Fair enough," Jed said.

The two hunkered down beside the dying fire to finish off the coffeepot. This time Fargo poured. Jed was the first to speak.

"Old son," Jed drawled, "last night I found out something: you and me got something in common."

"Make sense, Jed."

"Betty told me yer story. At the same time she came up with a description of that jasper you're huntin'. Ericson. Betty told me he's a redhead. Right?"

Fargo nodded.

"And he's got a girl in tow—a girl who's maybe a mite disturbed."

"I suppose there's a good chance of that," Fargo replied. "What are you gettin' at, Jed?"

"Fargo, I know where you can find that son of a bitch."

Fargo turned to look at Jed. The mountain man's words astonished him. Frowning, he said, "Now, how in the hell would you know that?"

"This Ericson you're lookin' for is the same bastard what drove me from my place. And I saw the girl he was with, too. Like I said, she wasn't takin' it so good."

"Slow down, Jed. Slow down. Let's have the whole story, one bite at a time."

With understandable bitterness, Jed told Fargo of the sudden appearance on horseback of a seemingly demented woman and described how Ericson had come up behind him and clubbed him with his revolver, then driven Jed from his valley, afoot and without firepower.

When he had finished, Fargo was convinced. He knew now where Red Ericson could be found. He and Jed stood up.

"All right, Jed. Where's this valley of yours?"

"North. I'd say a week's ride—maybe longer through this snow."

Fargo tossed the remains of his coffee into the campfire. "Then let's ride."

8

A day later they saw Indian signs. Nez Percé, both men agreed. They kept on, pushing deeper into the Bitterroots, grateful that the sky remained clear. Indeed, the weather had turned so unseasonably warm that the streams had lost most of their icy cover and were choked with running water. Mountain flowers, tricked by the steady sunlight, were blossoming in sunlit patches where the snow had melted.

The problem was the snow cover that remained. The sun glancing off the extensive snow fields caused both men to ride with their hat brims pulled well down over their faces, though this did little to shield their eyes from the unremitting glare. They camped just outside Jed's mountain valley a week later, and the next morning began their struggle up the mountainside to the high pass that allowed access to the valley.

The wet, melting snow was heavy and in spots dangerously slippery. As Fargo pulled his pinto up steep portions of the slope, it felt as if he were dragging behind him a team of oxen, so heavy was the going. Fortunately, despite the exertion, the wound in his side gave him no trouble.

By nightfall, they reached the pass and camped by a stream so swollen it was overflowing its banks, sending water creeping under the snow cover still bordering it. This made finding a suitable campsite close by the stream very difficult, and in addition they had a problem locating dry firewood. And once they got a fire going, it gave off so much smoke and so little fire they gave up trying to use it and stomped it out. That night they dined on dry sourdough biscuits washed down with icy water, and slept without a fire.

The next morning, from thin strips of wood and rawhide, they fashioned makeshift sunglasses and found that peering at the world through the narrow opening between the wood strips effectively shielded their eyes from the sun's glare. Then, keeping to the streambed, they rode on through the high pass. When they camped that night, Jed assured Fargo they would reach the valley by noon the next day.

Fargo accepted this news somberly. It had occurred to him by this time how impossible it would have been for him to have found this valley—and Red Ericson—if he had not had Jed Two Shoes to show him the way.

Just as Jed told him, a little before noon the following day both men were dismounting at the edge of a thick stand of pine while they gazed down at the valley. Jed had spoken of the place as a paradise. Now, as Fargo stood beside him looking down at its breathtaking sweep, he realized Jed had not exaggerated. This neatly enclosed world looked fresh and undefiled—the bright green of the timber standing out sharply against the carpet of snow, while above it the bright-blue firmament hung cloudless and pristine, like a newly washed window. This was how the world must have looked on the day of creation.

They mounted up and started down the steep slope. The scent of wet pine baking in the high sun filled the air with an intoxicating fragrance. Fargo could imagine what this valley would be like during the spring. In his mind'd eye he could see the boulder-strewn meadows ablaze with wild flowers—paintbrush and blue flax, thistles, and occasional sunbursts of yellow mariposa lillies.

That night they camped by the side of a roaring torrent fed by the melting snow fields above them. By noon of the next day they were well into the lower slopes, riding through stands of alder and cottonwoods, and across broad muddy meadows spotted by small, melting snow fields. As they pulled up beside a stream to camp for their noon meal, Jed held up his hand to caution Fargo.

"Just ahead of you," he said softly, without looking at Fargo. "In among those willows."

Fargo, in the act of dismounting, glanced toward the willows.

An enormous male grizzly was downwind of them. He had been feeding in the willow grove. In preparation for his winter sleep, he was in the process of piling on the tallow and had obviously gone a long way in that direction. He was the largest grizzly Fargo had ever seen.

At their approach, he had risen on his hind legs to gain a better view of the intruders. He was brownish yellow in color, except for a sizable hump on his back that was almost pure silver. His weak eyes were trying to make them out, his huge dish face still, alert. Only his nose twitched. Abruptly, he dropped onto all fours and shambled off in a deceptively swift, rolling gait.

Not until he was out of sight did Jed relax and turn to Fargo, a grin on his face. "That was Old Silver Hump. A real dandy, he is. He's gettin' bigger and sassier every year."

They both swung out of their saddles then and built a campfire. While they ate, Fargo could not help wondering if that granddaddy of all grizzlies might not be watching them.

"This here end of the valley is loaded with them big fellers," Jed said. "There's plenty of food for them up here, so they never messed with me. 'Course, every once in a while Old Silver Hump would rob one of my traps. But I never argued with him none about that. I always figured the valley was big enough for both of us."

"How far are we from your cabin?"

"We should make it before dark."

"Good."

Ericson was nervous. It was dusk and there was a curious hush in the air. He stepped to the cabin doorway and looked across the flat to the stream. It was free of ice now and he could hear its dim, constant roar, as he had all day. But that was the only familiar sound that came to him. About this time of day there usually came the anxious chirp of the chickadees or the long, haunting call of the wood thrush coming from deep within the timber above the cabin.

But this evening, nothing. Not a sound.

He glanced at the sky. There was not a trace of a cloud. The wind, unseasonably warm, had been from the south for almost a week now. He wondered how long this curious, unhealthy thaw would continue. He didn't like it. He wanted the snow to roar in and close off the valley again. He felt more secure, safer somehow, with the wind screaming through the pass, the fire roaring in his fireplace, the wolves howling outside.

He studied the timber farther up the valley. The nearest stand was only a hundred yards away. He thought he saw movement in it. He studied it for a moment or so. But he saw nothing further to arouse his suspicion and turned back into the cabin.

He was hungry, he realized.

Crouching in the corner by the fireplace, Cindy was still braiding her hair. A bitter flash of irritation swept over Ericson. Over and over, for weeks now, she had kept up this ceaseless braiding of her hair, humming tunelessly all the while.

"Cindy," he barked, "put the supper on! Some of that beaver-tail stew."

She got up instantly, as if his words had been a lash about her shoulders. Yet she did not look at him or in any other way indicate she had heard him. He watched her for a moment to make sure she was heading toward the stove, then stepped back outside the cabin.

This time he walked as far as the corral to gain a closer view of the pines. He still could not shake the uneasy feeling that he had earlier seen something moving in the timber. Leaning on the topmost timber, he studied the pines carefully. At last his patience was rewarded. He caught quick movement, a shadowy figure moving from tree to tree and the glint of gunmetal.

It was that old mountain man, the one he had driven from this valley. Of this Ericson had no doubt. He had been expecting the old fool to return in the spring. But this unexpected thaw had brought him sooner. His blood racing with eagerness, Ericson slipped quickly back to the cabin, ducked inside, and lifted his rifle down from the wall. Snatching up cartridges from a box on the mantel over the fireplace, he dropped them into the pocket of his buckskin jacket and hurried back out.

Crouching behind the corral, he loaded the rifle, slipped off the safety, and peered once more at the timber. But this time there was nothing to see. He rested his rifle on the corral's topmost pole while his eyes slowly searched the entire line of pines, especially where the flat met the slope. Abruptly, a ptarmigan and four fat chicks exploded out of a thicket on the border of the pines.

A smile on his face, Ericson aimed carefully at the thicket and sent a round into it. Then, reloading swiftly, he sent four more rounds into it. After that, he began to spray the area around the thicket, sending sprays of snow geysering into the air. He was enjoying himself immensely.

Fargo and Jed hugged the snow into which they had burrowed after the first shot. Cursing softly, Fargo turned his head to see how Jed was doing. Jed gazed back at him, his face grim as the rounds tore through the thicket's branches just above his head.

"Soon's the son of a bitch lets up," Fargo said, "I'll return his fire."

Jed nodded miserably. "That's my rifle he's usin', the son of a bitch."

The distance was too great for Jed's big Colt, a fact that had started him to muttering unhappily the moment Ericson opened up on them.

Abruptly, the firing ceased. Fargo peered up through the thicket. Ericson was heading back to the cabin.

Sitting up quickly, Fargo caught Ericson in his sights and squeezed the trigger. But his haste went against him. He missed, as a portion of the coral fence went flying. Ericson ducked his head and lit out for the cabin. Before Fargo could reload and fire, Ericson was inside the cabin.

"Shit," said Fargo.

"Looks like we can't count on surprisin' him now," Jed remarked.

Fargo just nodded bitterly.

The two men had planned to free Cindy Talcott before opening up on Ericson. But any chance of that was gone now. Ericson knew they were out there, and Fargo was almost certain Ericson would use Cindy for cover when Fargo and Jed closed in.

"How the hell do you suppose the son of a bitch knew we was out here?" Jed asked.

"That family of ptarmigans we flushed."

"That told him where we were, all right. But the thing is, he must've already been onto us by then."

Fargo saw no sense in debating it. The thing to do now was flush the son of a bitch. He was about to suggest the two of them split up and come at the cabin from different directions when both men saw the cabin door open.

Cindy Talcott was pushed into the doorway. Fargo winced at her appearance. Even at this distance, he could see how much she had deteriorated. She stood in the cabin doorway for only a moment. Then Ericson pushed her all the way out, following close behind her.

He had his left arm around her waist, and in his right hand he held his knife, the point of it thrust well up under Cindy's chin.

"I got this here crazy woman, old man," Ericson called. "I'll kill her if you don't step out and throw your gun down."

"Stay down," Jed told Fargo. "He knows it's me come back, but he ain't seen you yet."

"The girl looks bad. Very bad."

"Do you think he'll kill her?"

"Yes," Fargo said bitterly. "If he has to, he won't hesitate. My God, look at her."

Jed nodded. "She's tetched, Fargo. I noticed that, first thing. I seen the same thing with women taken by the Indians. They just can't take the abuse."

"Come on, old man," Ericson called. "I know you're out there. I saw you in the pines. If you're hit, just call out. Maybe I'll send my nurse out to see you." He laughed.

"Keep him talking," Fargo told Jed. "Stall the son of a bitch."

"What're you gonna do?"

"Cut around behind the cabin. Take him by surprise."

"You better answer me, old man," Ericson shouted. "If you don't, I'll cut this woman's throat. It'll be your fault if I do."

As he spoke, Ericson thrust his knife's razor-sharp point into the flesh under Cindy's chin. A dark gout of blood spurted down her neck and into her bosom.

Jed groaned at the sight.

"Jesus, Fargo," he said. "I can't do it. I can't stall him. He's going to kill her right in front of us!"

Before Fargo could stop him, Jed got to his feet, pushed through the thicket, and hurried out onto the meadow toward Ericson.

"Let that woman be," Jed cried. "I'm alone. It's just me come back. No need for you to kill that woman."

"Drop that Colt!"

Obediently, Jed lifted the Walker Colt out of his belt and dropped it to the ground.

"Come closer!"

Jed walked across the flat toward him. Fargo cursed. He didn't trust Ericson, but he had to let Jed make his play. As long as Ericson had no idea Jed was not alone, Fargo still had the advantage of surprise.

Suddenly sheathing his knife, Ericson flung Cindy back into the cabin and drew his own six-gun. Smiling broadly, he pumped a quick shot at Jed. The mountain man staggered as the round caught him in the chest. He went down on one knee, then toppled into the snow.

The instant Ericson flung Cindy away from him, Fargo raised his rifle and sighted on Ericson through the bushes. But so shocked was he at the suddenness with which Jed was cut down that he paused momentarily. When he did fire, he succeeded only in shattering the cabin window beside Ericson. At once Ericson ducked back into the cabin and slammed the door behind him.

Jed sat up.

As Fargo watched in astonishment, Jed pushed himself to his feet and staggered back toward the thicket. Before he reached it, however, rifle fire from the cabin knocked him to his knees. Fargo raced out of the thicket toward Jed. When he reached him, Jed was sitting stiffly upright in the snow, a thin tracery of blood trickling out of his mouth. He had a dim, shocked look in his eyes as he gazed up at Fargo.

More rifle fire came from the cabin. Fargo flung Jed over his shoulder and turned for the timber. As he raced toward it, a steady rattle of gunfire followed him. Once safely in the trees, he lifted Jed onto his horse.

"You going to be able to stay in the saddle?" he asked Jed.

"Sure," the old man mumbled, his hand grasping clumsily at the reins.

"Okay, then. Follow me."

Fargo mounted up and rode back up through the timber until they found a dry spot in a meadow overlooking the valley some distance from the cabin.

Night was falling rapidly now, but the sky overhead was still light. Fargo lifted Jed down out of his saddle, propped him up against a tree, and built a campfire. Then he saw to the horses, after which he returned to Jed.

"How do you feel, Jed?"

Jed smiled slightly. "Like someone just pumped two slugs into me."

"You shouldn't have stepped out in plain sight like that."

"I was afraid he'd kill her. Did he?"

"No, not yet."

Jed began to shiver. Fargo took off his sheepskin jacket and threw it over the big mountain man's shoulders. "Let me get this fire built up some," he said. "Then I'll take a look at them wounds."

"No need for that," Jed whispered. "I'm dead, Fargo. He caught me good each time."

"Don't talk like that, damn it!"

"Listen, Fargo, it ain't so bad. I got back here to the valley, didn't I? And it's here I'll be buried. That's all I wanted, anyway."

"Just let me get this fire going. Soon's I get enough light, I'll be able to dig those slugs out."

"Sure, Fargo."

Working swiftly, Fargo built up the campfire, dipped his knife blade into the flames, then hurried over to Jed. The old man had leaned his head back against the tree and was looking up at the first stars gleaming in the evening sky. But Jed did not see a single one. He would never see another night sky again, not from this valley, not from this earth.

Fargo went back to the fire and sat down beside it.

For a long time he stared into the leaping flames. What he saw in them was the grinning, mocking face of Red Ericson.

As dawn broke over the valley, Fargo found a proper burial site for Jed Two Shoes on a rise flanked by tall pines. It afforded an unobstructed view of the snow-patched valley floor and the willow-bordered stream beyond. A long, low ridge separated this flat from the one the cabin bordered. As Fargo stood looking down at the stream cutting its dark passage through the snow, he thought he heard the sharp, distant slap of a beaver's tail.

Yes, this would do.

Fargo had little to dig with, mostly the barrel of his Sharps and his own two hands. Fortunately, the early snow cover had prevented the frost from setting up, and he was able to go deep enough to ensure that Jed would not be dug up by wolves or coyotes. Dressing Jed in his new buffalo coat and then wrapping him in his soogan, Fargo buried him in the trench. He covered him with pine branches and then with heavy rocks, working steadily until a waist-high cairn had been erected.

As he stood for a moment over Jed's grave, Fargo was filled with a rage he could barely contain. But at last he managed to dampen his powerful sorrow long enough to pray for the soul of Jed Two Shoes. But even as he spoke his clumsy prayer, he knew it wasn't really needed. There was no way in hell a man like Jed Two Shoes was going to be denied paradise.

A moment later, as Fargo swung aboard his pinto,

he was startled to see the same grizzly Jed Two Shoes had pointed out to him earlier. The bear was standing on an outcropping of rock on the slope above Fargo. He was less than twenty yards away and close enough for Fargo to see the glint in his intelligent dark eyes. As he remained upright, he held his front paws out before him almost in an attitude of prayer—as if he, too, were saying good-bye to the old mountain man.

Old Silver Hump, Jed had called him. The bear had known Jed Two Shoes, had become accustomed to his scent. Perhaps he had also come to like the old mountain man.

Raising his arm in greeting to the magnificent beast, Fargo turned his pinto about and rode back down through the pines. Halfway down the slope, he turned to look back. Old Silver Hump was down on all fours, shambling toward what appeared to be his den, a dark hollow staring out from under a ledge.

When Fargo reached the flat below, he looked back for one last glimpse of Jed's grave site. Old Silver Hump had vanished.

9

Red Ericson had been prowling about the cabin since dawn as Cindy finished packing their gear. He hated what he had to do. The thought of leaving this valley filled him with a terrible fury. But the truth of the matter was that for the first time in his life Red Ericson felt true fear.

He had killed the old trapper, the man he had dispossessed. Of that he was reasonably sure. But it was the one with him he wanted—the man he thought Cindy had already killed. He had recognized him the moment he darted from cover to carry off the wounded trapper.

Fargo.

Yet, how could this be? He had seen Cindy cut him down with the loaded six-gun he had given her for just that purpose. Then he had seen her standing over him, filling him with lead. He had bent close and noted the blood covering Fargo's shattered skull.

Later, as he had ridden off, he had watched the cabin go up in flames with Fargo still inside, locked inside.

In the gathering dusk last night, perhaps his eyes had played a trick on him. Maybe it was not Fargo he had seen running out from the thicket. But no, Ericson could not mistake that man. Only on Fargo had he seen such powerful shoulders. And only someone as powerful as Fargo could have hefted that mountain man so casually onto his back and raced with him into the timber.

It was Skye Fargo, all right.

Ericson took a deep breath and went to the cabin doorway. Before opening the door, he glanced back at Cindy. She was packing furiously, her lips moving silently. He could barely hear the low mutter of her insane jabber. Before her on the bed was the gear she had spent the night packing for him.

"I'm goin' to saddle up the horses," he told her. "Stay here until I'm ready for you."

She did not turn her head to look at him. But he knew from experience she had heard him perfectly and would do as he said. Rifle at the ready, he stepped carefully out through the doorway. The sight of the empty flat did not comfort him, nor did the silent pine forest clothing the slopes of the valley. Fargo was out there somewhere right now, he knew. Waiting. Watching.

Well, Ericson had no intention of staying in this cabin any longer. With Fargo commanding the slopes, Ericson was a sitting duck. Before Fargo made his next move, Ericson and his woman would be on their way out of this valley, and once they reached the timber, it would be as easy for him to bushwhack Fargo as it would be for Fargo to bushwhack him. And he always had the woman to use as a shield.

Leaving the door open behind him, he started for the barn. He had almost reached it when the first rifle shot came from the slope above it. At once he ducked back behind the cabin and peered up at the pines, hoping to catch a puff of smoke to sight on.

Then he noticed the feebly thrashing horse in the far corner of the corral. A second shot broke the morning stillness, and this time Ericson heard the bullet's impact as it struck his second horse.

Fargo was shooting their horses!

A moment later the third shot took down his pack horse.

In a transport of fury, Ericson fired up the slope into the pines. With trembling fingers he reloaded, fired again, and reloaded. He kept on firing until the breech began to heat up dangerously. Only then did he hold up, suddenly aware of his vulnerability.

Without horses he was trapped up here in this high valley, hundreds of miles from a trading post or town. Oh, that dirty son of a bitch! What kind of a man could calmly pick off horseflesh like that?

Abruptly, Ericson realized that for some time there had been no more rifle fire from the pines. Fargo could be anywhere. He could be slipping down through the pines at that very moment, coming at the cabin from the other side. Ericson turned and raced back. A rifle shot came from the timber in front of the cabin. An enormous chunk of wood leapt out of the door frame an inch over Ericson's head.

He flung himself into the cabin and kicked the door shut.

Sick at heart, Fargo came to a halt in the pines above the cabin. Each round he had put into the horses seemed to have struck him as well.

It had been the toughest thing he had ever had to do, but Fargo could think of no other way to prevent Ericson from escaping the valley. With Cindy at his side to shield Ericson, Fargo would have been unable to stop him from riding off, and once Ericson reached the timber, there was no saying how far he would get. This weather would not hold much longer. As soon as it began to snow again and winter finally returned, Fargo risked losing track of Ericson—and Cindy Talcott—completely. It would not be easy to find them again.

But Ericson was not going anywhere. Not now. There was only one punishment a man truly dreaded in this country, and that was going afoot.

Fargo started to work his way down through the timber. He was now about to flush the son of a bitch from his hole. And he had a pretty good idea how to do that.

If, that is, he could find enough dry brush.

The smell of smoke brought Ericson alert in an instant. He was sitting with his back to the cabin wall, facing the door, his rifle in his lap. He had expected Fargo to start peppering the cabin, to shoot out the other window and maybe rush the cabin.

But it was fire instead he was using. Something—brush, probably—was burning against the rear of

144

the cabin. Thick smoke was pulsing through the cracks and from under the floor. Already his eyes were beginning to smart.

Cindy began to laugh. It was more a demented chuckle, and it was unsettling. She had long since given up trying to attack him. Instead, whenever he found himself in any kind of difficulty, she began this creepy chuckling.

He got quickly to his feet and regarded her blackly. Abruptly, she turned her head and stared directly at him. Her eyes had the light of madness in them.

"Get up," he told her. "Get up, damn you! We got to get out of here."

She came to her feet, a gaunt, grinning scarecrow of a woman.

"Come on! Get over here."

She walked over obediently. He grabbed her arm as soon as she was close enough and drew her close to him.

"Now, you listen, and listen good," he told her. "You stick close by me, you understand? If you try to break away, I'll slice your grinning head off."

She stared at him, unblinking through the growing cloud of smoke.

"Damn it! Did you hear me?"

Cindy began to chuckle.

Ericson yanked her toward the door, rifle in hand His six-gun, every chamber loaded, was in his holster. Squinting through the acrid smoke, he stopped in front of the door and glanced back at the wall. Tiny flames—like a million eyes—were flickering along its length just above the floorboards.

He turned back to Cindy. "Open the door and step out," he told her. "And remember what I said. Don't try to make a break for it."

Cindy pulled open the door and stepped out, Ericson right behind her, his hand still holding her arm in a viselike grip. Behind them, the sudden draft caused by the open door sucked the smoke out the door after them, enveloping them both for a minute. Glancing back, Ericson saw the flames along the rear wall leaping into life. There was no going back now.

"Get down," Ericson told Cindy, yanking her to the ground beside him.

He had expected Fargo to open up on him the moment he stepped out of the cabin. But Fargo had held his fire because of Cindy. Now, Ericson realized, he could use the thick smoke piling out through the doorway as a screen.

Keeping his head down, he started to crawl toward the corral, pulling Cindy along with him. He made certain she was on the outside and he was in the inside, just inches from the cabin wall. He intended to use the corral railing and barn for cover.

Cindy went along with him, utterly silent now, which was almost as unnerving as her earlier idiot laughter had been.

Abruptly, the barn erupted into flames as the old weathered boards caught with fierce suddenness. Ericson swore. He was caught between two blazing buildings. By this time he had reached the corral. He pulled himself and then Cindy under the lowest pole. Taking cover behind the carcass of one of the dead horses, he lay there with sweaty palms, waiting for Fargo to make his next move.

Furious though he was, Ericson was far from panic. He had a perfect shield in Cindy, and with her by his side to assure him safe passage, he would soon be on his way, riding that fool Fargo's own mount out of here.

Fargo was lying behind a patch of grass less than a hundred yards from the cabin, partially shielded by a low snowdrift. Waiting for Ericson to make his break from the cabin, he pulled back the hammer and trained his Sharps on the cabin door. The dried pine needles and branches he had spent most of the morning digging up and piling along the back of the cabin had caught slowly. But now they were making up for lost time. It would not be long before the barn went up as well.

Watching the smoke pump up from behind the cabin, Fargo wondered if Ericson had seen enough of him the day before to realize who he was. He hoped so. He wanted Ericson to know it was Fargo who was after him.

Suddenly the door was pulled open and Ericson pushed Cindy out ahead of him. Grimly, Fargo held his fire. He had lost a gamble. Had Ericson stepped out first, Fargo would have blown his head off.

As Ericson and Cindy crawled along the ground toward the barn, he kept his sights on the two bobbing heads, praying that Cindy would jump up and make a break for it. The barn went up with a roar, kicking embers high into the sky. Ericson paused for only a moment, and kept on toward the corral. When he pulled Cindy down behind the carcass of one of the three dead horses, Fargo felt bitter frustration.

All Fargo could do was wait and pray that Cindy might break away. He wiped the palm of his hand dry, then trained the Sharps on the dead horse. Perhaps if he sent a few rounds into the carcass, it might unnerve Ericson enough to make him leave Cindy behind and run for it.

Then, without warning, Ericson stood up, pulling Cindy up in front of him. Fargo cursed and lowered his rifle.

"You out there, Fargo?" Ericson cried.

So Ericson knew it was Fargo, did he? Good.

"I know you're out there," Ericson insisted. "And I know why you didn't shoot just now. Now listen to me! If you shoot me, you better be sure I'm dead with that one shot. If you don't—before I die, I'll take Cindy with me!"

Fargo frowned, but kept his silence. He saw no sense in giving away his position now.

Abruptly, the man shoved Cindy ahead of him as he left the corral and started foward across the flat, heading toward a low ridge. He was not at all gentle with Cindy as he dragged her, stumbling and lurching, along with him. Twice Fargo brought up his Sharps to try a head shot. But each time he lowered his rifle. Ericson was smart enough to keep his head down, and though Fargo trusted his Sharps, he dared not take the chance of missing Ericson and hitting Cindy instead.

At last he rose from the snow and watched as Ericson and Cindy disappeared into the wooded ridge. Then he turned and ran back into the pines for his pinto.

Mounted, Fargo tracked Ericson for the rest of that afternoon. On those occasions when Fargo glimpsed them through the trees, he saw how Ericson kept his left arm wrapped tightly around Cindy's waist. The two moved almost as one person. Over and over to himself, Fargo whispered for Cindy to break away from her captor, as if somehow his words could reach out and galvanize her.

But soon he realized that Cindy was barely conscious of the world around her. At times he was close enough to hear her uttering sounds and cries he could barely understand. Every now and then she would break into a kind of toneless singing. And all this while, without offering the slightest resistance, she allowed herself to be pulled brutally along by Ericson.

Cindy, Fargo realized finally, was not going to be able to help him.

Her mind had gone completely. The Cindy Talcott whom Fargo had spoken to in the Deer Lodge saloon—her eyes glowing with happiness at the prospect of her upcoming marriage—was dead, as surely as if her cold body were rotting in a pine box seven feet under. The pitifully gaunt frame being hauled cruelly through these woods no longer contained the soul of Cindy Talcott. An impostor animated her body—a filthy, scrawny madwoman.

As Jed Two Shoes had already observed, she had become like those women taken in raids by Indian war parties. The very young girls were sometimes able to adapt, but the older women almost always went wild with the strangeness and privation of their new life and the brutal way in which they were raped over and over by their fierce Indian masters.

Like those poor, ravaged women, Cindy had simply been unable to accept the cruel usage put to her by Ericson.

Toward the close of the day, Fargo pulled up and watched from less than fifty yards as Ericson selected a campsite on a meadow beside a stream. This entire flat had lost its snow cover, and he had selected a dry knoll. Dismounting, Fargo tethered his pinto to a sapling, then stole closer to the edge of the timber.

Crouching down in a clump of juniper, Fargo thumbed back the hammer on his Sharps and waited.

Ericson was bent over the few dry branches and twigs he had found about the knoll and was working hard to get a fire started. Cindy, evidently on orders from Ericson, was ranging a few feet about the knoll, picking up more kindling for the fire.

Fargo's chance had come.

He raised his Sharps. Cindy paused between Fargo and Ericson to pick up a dried branch. Fargo waited for her to move on so that he would have a clear shot, one that would make it impossible for Ericson to carry out his threat to retaliate on Cindy.

Then Ericson saw his danger.

"Get back here," he barked to Cindy, swinging up his rifle and peering quickly around.

Cindy turned as if struck, her arms heavy with kindling. Obediently, still keeping between Fargo and Ericson, she started back to Ericson.

Fargo stood up in plain sight. "No, Cindy," he cried "No! Don't go back! Run! Get away!"

She pulled up in some confusion and turned to look back at Fargo, a dim comprehension on her face. Unsheathing his knife, Ericson broke for Cindy. Darting to one side, Fargo tucked ths Sharps into his shoulder and sighted along the barrel. But even as he caught Ericson in his sights, Ericson flung himself at Cindy, tackling her from behind. She went down heavily, the wood she had gathered scattering before her.

Fargo dared not shoot now. As he lowered his rifle and ducked back behind a tree, Ericson dragged her to her feet and held her up in front of him.

"You came back from the dead, Fargo!" he called. "But it won't do you no good! I got her, and there ain't a thing you can do about it."

His knife was in his right hand, its gleaming point digging cruelly into the flesh under her chin.

"Now I'm gonna tell you what to do," Ericson continued. "Drop that rifle and step out from behind that tree. Do it, or I'll slit her throat. And if you don't think I mean it, watch!"

He thrust the knife brutally upward. Cindy tilted her head back and Fargo saw a neck so filthy it had a sooty cast to it.

"You heard me, Fargo," Ericson began to drag Cindy back to his campsite near the knoll. "Drop that rifle and step out from cover. Do it now or I'll kill her!"

"You kill her and you'll be just as dead a second later."

Ericson had almost reached the campsite—and his

151

rifle. "Maybe!" he yelled back at Fargo. "So what do I lose by taking her first? Sooner or later you're going to bushwhack me. I ain't got no choice."

Cindy began to struggle. Ericson thrust the knife in deeper to quiet her. Instantly, the blade was covered with blood. With a sudden screech, high and unnatural, Cindy turned finally on her tormentor.

Fargo had difficulty following what happened next.

As Cindy turned on Ericson, she swung her head so violently around she caused the blade in Ericson's hand to slice suddenly, cruelly upward, severing her jugular. A thick freshet of blood exploded down the front of her dress. Her screech died abruptly.

In that instant, she was dead.

Throwing Cindy's limp body from him, Ericson flung himself to the ground and reached out for his rifle. Profoundly shaken at the horror of what he had just witnessed, Fargo fired at the scrambling figure. But his bullet missed as Ericson hauled up his rifle and returned Fargo's fire.

The slug pounded into the tree inches above Fargo's head. Ducking back into the timber, Fargo drew his Colt.

By then Ericson—his own six-gun drawn—was splashing across the shallow stream, sending a steady volley toward Fargo in the trees. Crouching, Fargo returned the fire, but the distance was too great. Swiftly reloading the Sharps, he slammed the stock up into his shoulder.

An instant before Fargo caught him in his sights, Ericson vanished into the timber on the far side of the stream.

10

Numbly, Fargo lowered his Sharps and looked out at Cindy's pitiful, sprawling figure. For him to try to retrieve her body for burial at this time would be foolhardy. From the cover of the timber on the other side of the stream, Ericson's rifle could cut him down easily.

Fargo slipped farther back into the timber. Untying his pinto, he vaulted into the saddle and made for higher ground away from the stream. As he rode, he was calmed somewhat by his clear understanding of the task that lay before him. Now it was just Ericson and him. Cindy was free of him—free at last.

Night was falling fast. He found a campsite above the valley close by an outcropping of rock with loose shale covering the ground all about him. He made a dry camp and slept with his Colt in his hand, secure in the knowledge that somewhere in the valley below him Red Ericson would not dare to sleep.

When he awoke in the chill of dawn, he lit no fire and ate a cold breakfast. Then he mounted up and rode back to where he had left Cindy's body. He did not stop, but continued on across the stream. He had no difficulty picking up Ericson's tracks, and a mile or so farther on, he saw clearly where Ericson had spent the night. When it became obvious that Ericson was heading straight for the low pass due west that led from the valley, he turned his pinto about and rode back for Cindy's body.

Wrapping her remains in his slicker, he slung it over his pommel and rode back to Jed Two Shoes' grave site. He buried her alongside Jed, then started back down the slope, glancing back once to see if Old Silver Hump had emerged from his den to watch this time.

He had not.

By noon Fargo had picked up Ericson's trail. The man was not used to walking, especially in high-heeled riding boots. From the look of his footprints, the Trailsman could see how much the man was suffering. This did not displease Fargo. The important thing, however, was that Ericson was still making a beeline for the pass.

Fargo cut wide of Ericson's tracks, gained the wooded slopes above the valley, and rode west until he judged himself to be at least a mile or so ahead of him. Dismounting, he tethered his pinto out of sight in a stand of aspen, then lugged his Sharps over to a large pine, from beside which he had an unobstructed view of the exposed flat beneath him and of the stream slicing through it.

Fargo cut himself a shooting stick and stuck it firmly into the spongy ground before him. Sitting cross-legged on a damp patch of grass, he rested the Sharps' barrel in the crotch of the stick. Then he took out a handful of cartridges. He selected one and slipped it into the breech and cranked up the trigger guard. Then he placed the rest of the cartridges down onto a flat rock beside him, and waited.

In due time Ericson emerged from the timberline bordering the flat. He was in such a hurry he did not look to the left or right as he plunged on across the flat. As Fargo had surmised, he was limping painfully by this time.

Fargo waited until Ericson was in the middle of the flat before he tucked the stock into his shoulder and eased back the hammer. He estimated the distance as a little over four hundred yards—not a difficult shot for the Sharps. Considering the wind and allowing for drift, Fargo squeezed the trigger.

The slopes around him rocked with the detonation. A second later, a chunk of turf just in front of Ericson flew into the air. Ericson scrambled to a halt. Going swiftly down on one knee, he brought his rifle up and peered at the slope in Fargo's direction.

Swiftly, Fargo levered out the empty cartridge, reloaded, and placed another round at Ericson's feet. The man scrambled back a few feet, then turned and began to run away from the slope. Fargo's next round whistled over his shoulder, plowing into a small snowbank just ahead of him. Ericson pulled up so suddenly his legs went out from under him.

Scrambling to his feet, he tried this time to hobble back the way he had come. Calmly reloading, Fargo placed the next round inches in front of him. As the turf exploded, Ericson swerved, slipped, and fell again.

Fargo swept the remaining cartridges off the rock. Then he stepped out onto the slope and waved his rifle over his head. "Up here, Ericson," he yelled.

Ericson saw him at once. Snatching his rifle, he brought it up to his shoulder. Fargo knew the man's rifle and had a pretty good idea of its range. He pulled up his shooting stick and, carrying the Sharps in the crook of his arm, angled swiftly down the slope toward the flat.

On his feet now, Ericson fired up the slope at Fargo, reloaded swiftly, then fired again.

Fargo ignored him as he kept going until he estimated himself to be just out of range of Ericson's rifle. Then he planted his shooting stick again and settled down behind it. Much closer now on the flat below him, Ericson went down on knee, steadied himself, aimed very carefully, and fired. Ten yards below Fargo, Ericson's round blew away a hunk of rock. Fargo was impressed. Considering the distance and the rifle Ericson was using, it was an excellent shot.

A grim smile on his hawklike face, Fargo calmly reloaded his Sharps. He judged himself to be about two hundred yards from Ericson. At that distance he knew he could clip the whiskers off a muskrat. He thumbed back the hammer, sighted carefully, and squeezed the trigger. The rifle leapt suddenly out of Ericson's hand. Ericson grabbed his hand and jumped back, his cry coming faintly up to Fargo. Reloading swiftly, Fargo fired again. This time the force of the fifty-caliber slug caused the rifle to kick up off the ground. When it came down, the barrel flipped in one direction, the stock in the other.

Ericson, still holding his left hand, made no effort to run. Instead, he stood boldly, facing Fargo. "All right, you bastard," he cried. "Kill me and be done with it!"

Fargo got up and cupped his hand to his mouth. "Heave that Colt up here,' he shouted.

Ericson drew the Colt from his holster and flung it as far up the slope as he could.

"You still got that knife, Ericson?"

"Sure," the man cried back hopefully. Pulling the blade from its sheath he brandished it and took a step toward Fargo.

"Good," Fargo called back to him. "You'll be needing it. Now, go on back to the cabin. I'll be waiting there for you."

"No, Fargo! Settle it now. Here."

"You heard me."

"No!"

Fargo sat back down behind the stick, reloaded calmly, aimed, and fired. The round plowed a furrow in the ground between Ericson's feet.

"Start back, Ericson. Now!"

Ericson raised his fist to Fargo. Even from this distance Fargo could see the taut lividness of his expression. "Damn your eyes! All right, I'll see you at the cabin. I'll be waitin'."

Ericson hobbled toward the pines and a moment later disappeared into them. Fargo moved back up the slope, dropped the Sharps into his scabbard, and swung up onto his pinto. Keeping to the timber, he cut due west, heading away from the cabin. Slowly, steadily, he kept going, the twin peaks marking the western pass opening before him.

By late afternoon, he had set up his forked stick once more, this time on a grassy ledge above the narrow trail that cut up through the pass. An hour before sundown, he smiled.

Far below him, Ericson appeared, struggling up the trail. Just as Fargo had expected, once in the cover of the trees, Ericson had doubled back and continued on toward the pass. Fargo did not blame Ericson for not wanting to go back to the cabin. He would have tried the same thing himself.

As Ericson climbed the trail, he labored painfully. Fargo had no difficulty imagining how footsore Ericson must be by then. The man had obviously been pushing himself to the limit.

When Ericson was less than a hundred yards distant, Fargo's first shot struck the trail in front of him. Thunderstruck, Ericson glanced frantically about him. Fargo fired again. This time he took a crease out of Ericson's right thigh.

The man spun to the ground, howling.

A third bullet struck the ground inches from Ericson's face, splattering him with mud and pulverized rock. Ericson began digging frantically at his eyes.

Fargo stood up in plain view.

"Ericson," he called down, "listen to me!"

Still on the ground, Ericson craned his neck to

stare up at his tormentor. "You bastard," he called hoarsely.

"The next round could just as easily go through your head," Fargo told him, his voice cold.

Instinctively, Ericson ducked his head.

"Or you can go back to the cabin like I told you and wait for me," Fargo told him. "And while you're waiting, sharpen that long knife of yours. The choice is up to you. Just remember. It don't matter what you try, you can't escape me or this valley. I can ride rings around you."

"Damn you," Ericson snarled. "Why not end it here?"

"I don't want to!"

Ericson's shoulders slumped wearily. He knew further argument would be hopeless.

"Camp below for the night," Fargo instructed him. "In the morning, go back. And follow close by the stream. You won't see me. But I'll be keeping you in sight."

Ericson pushed himself erect and stumbled painfully back down the trail to the flat below. Fargo watched him go for a moment, then turned and climbed up the steep slope to where he had left his pinto.

Fargo slept within sight of the trail. It was not a full, deep sleep, more like a series of catnaps. And he kept his Colt in his hand, cocked and with the safety off. But as he had surmised, Ericson was simply too disheartened and exhausted to search the slopes for Fargo's campsite or to try to make another break through the pass.

As dawn lightened the sky over the valley, Fargo watched Erickson pick his way back down to the stream. Staying in the wooded slopes above him, Fargo kept the man in sight all that morning. Ericson followed Fargo's instructions to the letter, keeping close by the stream as he trudged doggedly back the way he had come.

Once Fargo was certain Ericson was not going to try anything foolish, he spurred ahead, and an hour or so later he came out onto the slope above the cabin. Descending to it, he searched through the barn's blackened ruin until he found what he was looking for: a long strand of rawhide. Next, he poked about until he discovered a length of wood long enough to serve as a handle. To this he fastened the rawhide. When he was finished, he had what amounted to a crude, but effective whip.

Then he waited. By midafternoon, Ericson strode out of the woods close by the stream. Fargo mounted up and rode out to meet him.

Ericson pulled up as Fargo neared him, his knife brandished. There was a bloody bandage wrapped tightly around his thigh. The big fellow was a wonder, Fargo admitted to himself grudgingly. Despite the flesh wound, close by the same spot as his earlier knife wound, Ericson seemed to have recovered his stamina as well as his fury during his long grueling trek back to this flat.

Fargo pulled the pinto to a halt and dismounted, his Colt out, the muzzle leveled on Ericson.

"Now?" Ericson asked, his face watchful, his red-rimmed eyes ablaze with hatred. "You comin' at me now, Fargo? Where's your knife?"

"Not now, Ericson," Fargo told him. "Just let me have your boots, your hat, and that deerskin jacket."

"What the hell?"

"Just do as I say," Fargo told him, cocking the six-gun.

Bewildered by the request, Ericson kicked off his boots and shrugged out of his jacket. Then he flung his hat to the ground.

"Stand back," Fargo told him.

As Ericson moved back, Fargo picked up the man's clothing and mounted up again. Flinging the deerskin jacket over the pommel, he looked down at Ericson.

"I said you would have a chance to fight for your life, Ericson," he told the big man. "And I meant it. It won't be much of a chance, but it's more than you deserve. I suggest you begin to sharpen that knife of yours. It won't be a defensless woman's throat you'll be slicing this time."

"What the hell're you up to?" Ericson demanded.

Fargo smiled thinly, his lake-blue eyes glinting icily. "I'll bring these here clothes back to you before nightfall."

Then he turned the pinto and rode off.

Afoot, wearing Ericson's hat, Fargo approached the mouth of Old Silver Hump's den. Ericson's deerskin shirt he had tied around his waist. Draped about his neck from a length of rawhide were Ericson's boots. The fierce stench from Ericson's unwashed body permeated the shirt, and it seemed to Fargo that all the unwashed feet in Christiandom had at one time or another worn Ericson's boots.

His Sharps at the ready, Fargo entered the cave. He took a few steps, then waited for his eyes to get accustomed to the dimness. When they did, he became aware of the smell of bear, and also the smell of bat. He moved in still farther, then held up and waited—a primitive, root-deep alarm ringing deep inside him. This was no place for anyone on two legs.

He heard a dim snuffling sound, like someone wiping a runny nose. At the same time a great dark figure materialized out of the gloom just ahead of him. Slowly, Fargo moved back. The bear followed. Fargo had invaded his den, his refuge for the coming winter, and he did not like that. Not one bit. By the time Fargo had reached the cavern entrance, the enormous grizzly was down on all fours, gathering himself to charge.

Fargo broke quickly for the pinto, waiting for him not ten yards from the cave entrance. Leaping astride the pony, he drove his Sharps down into his scabbard and snatched up the whip he had fashioned just as Old Silver Hump charged from the cave.

Fargo spurred down through the pines, the huge grizzly crashing down the slope after him. When Fargo reached the flat, he turned the pinto about and held up. Old Silver Hump broke from the timber a few moments later and lumbered furiously toward him. Fargo felt the pinto trembling under him as the bear got closer. Old Silver Hump wasn't really angry yet, just intent on giving Fargo a warning he would not soon forget. As he ambled closer, the bear's weak eyes could tell him little, but his sensitive nose was certainly offended by the awful stench emanating from Red Ericson's garments.

Pulling up about twenty yards from Fargo, the huge bear sat suddenly back on his haunches, his small eyes peering at Fargo, his nose sniffing the air unhappily. The bear was puzzled. Why had Fargo pulled up? he appeared to be wondering. Why was this foul-smelling horseman not fleeing in terror from his fearsome charge?

Abruptly, Fargo spurred back toward the bear. The grizzly reared up onto his hind legs and uttered a loud *whoof!* in warning. But Fargo kept coming. At the last possible moment, he veered away and slashed down with his crude rawhide whip. It snapped cruelly across the grizzly's sensitive snout.

The grizzly's roar of outrage was awesome. It shattered the wilderness. As Fargo turned the pinto and loped swiftly away from the beast, he almost lost control of the pony, so frantic was his mount to gain distance from the enraged grizzly. Fargo managed to settle the pinto into a steady gallop, then glanced back. Losing ground only slowly, the bear was still charging full tilt after him.

Fargo tucked the whip into his belt and gave the pinto full rein as he galloped across the flat. Far to his right was the low timbered ridge separating this flat from the flat where Ericson waited. Fargo slowed down and glanced back. Then he pulled up. The bear had slowed also, but he was still coming. Fargo patted the pinto's neck and let him blow some. Stamping his feet nervously, the Ovaro flicked his tail. Fargo spoke softly, calmly to him. It was obvious the pinto did not like this game at all.

When Fargo judged the bear was close enough, he pulled out the whip again and loped back toward the oncoming bear. As Fargo got closer, he lifted the pinto to a gallop. The bear pulled up hastily and this time watched in some confusion as Fargo bore down on him.

But his confusion lasted only a moment. With a defiant, shattering roar, the huge grizzly accepted Fargo's challenge, put his massive head down, and charged. Fargo kept coming. Only at the last moment did he veer off, again coiling the whip around the bear's snout. As Fargo swept on past the enraged bear, he pulled the whip back, then circled the infuriated beast, driving him into a fine frenzy as he kept himself and the pinto just out of reach of the grizzly's slashing claws.

At last, whipping off Ericson's hat, Fargo leaned far out of the saddle and slapped at the bear's head with it. With a lightninglike swipe of his taloned paw, the bear tore the hat from Fargo's grasp and in a titanic fury ripped it to shreds. While the bear was thus venting his rage, Fargo pulled out his whip and snapped the rawhide tip once more around the beast's tender snout.

The bear's anguished roar deafened Fargo and nearly turned his pinto silly with fear. Snorting and rearing wildly, the pony's eyes started out of his head, but Fargo managed to gather the pinto under him, then let him out. With a charge born of simple panic, the pony bolted back across the meadow, the bear in hot pursuit.

By then, Fargo was galloping straight toward the ridge. Only a few yards from it, he managed to pull up the unhappy pinto and wait for the bear to get closer. As soon as he had, Fargo spurred his pony past the lunging grizzly, wheeled, and lashed out once more. The whip crackled about the bear's head like something alive, its quick, stinging bite tearing repeatedly at the animal's head and snout. The maddened grizzly charged Fargo again and again, his roars of outrage shattered the air. But each time Fargo was able to spin the pinto away.

At last the pony reached his limit and began to buck under Fargo. The second time he did so, Fargo let the bear pull the whip from his grasp, then wheeled his pinto and galloped straight onto the ridge. He looked back. The grizzly was keeping up, perhaps even gaining a little.

The pinto was going on sheer terror by this time. Foam flecked his jaws. His eyes were wild, bulging from their sockets. As he galloped across the timbered ridge, Fargo could hear the enraged bear behind him, crashing through the brush like some fearsome land leviathan. Once they crossed the ridge, Fargo gave the pinto his head. Though the bear began to fall behind, he was still coming, his pace not diminishing in the slightest.

Dimly visible at the far end of the flat, Fargo saw the remains of the cabin. Straight ahead of him was the stream where Ericson was waiting. As Fargo galloped closer, he caught sight of Ericson scrambling to his feet. A smile of anticipation creased the big redhead's face. Ericson was ready and eager for battle.

At the last minute, Fargo turned the pinto aside, then flung Ericson's boots and deerskin shirt to the ground at his feet.

In some astonishment Ericson looked down at the shirt and boots. "Hey," he called stupidly as Fargo galloped off, "where's my hat?"

It was getting colder. Ericson wasted no time slipping into his shirt and then pulling on his boots. He was angry Fargo had kept his hat—and also somewhat confused. When was that crazy son of a bitch going to come at him for the showdown he had promised?

The last time the two men had squared off, Ericson had gotten the worst of it. But not this time, by Jesus! No, sir! Not this time!

A thunderous roar came from Ericson's right. He turned his head. A huge grizzly was shambling across the flat toward him. Ericson groaned. This was the biggest goddamn bear Ericson had ever seen in his life. Though he had glimpsed a few of the valley's grizzlies from a distance, he had never seen this one.

In that instant he realized what Fargo had been up to all this time—and why he had let him keep his knife. This was the fighting chance Fargo had promised him. With a weary fatalism, Ericson unsheathed his skinning knife and turned to face the onrushing juggernaut. He was a dead man and he knew it.

Abruptly, the grizzly shambled to a halt. Then he reared up onto his hind legs and roared once more. At this distance Ericson could see tiny flecks of blood on the bear's snout as the animal's nose tested the air for Ericson's scent. Then the bear slammed down onto his forepaws and charged. Heavy and cummbersome though he appeared, the huge animal covered the distance between them with startling swiftness.

With a roar of his own, Ericson stepped forward to meet the grizzly. By the time he reached Ericson, the bear was upright, his teeth and gums and red tongue visible as he snarled and raked downward with his paw. Ericson felt a terrific blow strike his left shoulder, numbing it completely. But he ignored it, stepped in closer, and plunged his knife repeatedly into the side of the grizzly's neck, probing for the jugular.

The grizzly gave a shattering bellow and staggered back. Ericson pulled the knife free and stepped in close again. This time he plunged the knife into the animal's massive chest, driving it in up to the hilt. With a violent shake, the bear bellowed again and took another step back, the sudden movement ripping the knife from Ericson's grasp.

Ericson rocked back. But the great beast followed him and flung both forepaws around him. Ericson felt the bear's claws digging into his back as the bear crushed him. One by one, Ericson heard his ribs snap. The bear's breath seared his face. At the same time, Ericson became aware of a suffocating fountain of hot blood pouring over his face and chest and realized dimly that his earlier knife thrusts must have found the bear's jugular.

He felt a momentary pride and exultation. The bear didn't know it yet, but he was dead. With only his skinning knife, Ericson had killed himself a grizzly!

His exultation did not last long, however. It was replaced by the sudden awareness of excruciating pain. He was being shaken and cuffed about like a rag doll in the teeth of a puppy. He felt himself slammed to the ground, picked up, then hurled back onto the ground again. He felt dimly the grizzly's jaws as they crunched down into his right hip.

Then all sensation faded as the infuriated beast continued to shake and buffet him.

Long after Ericson ceased struggling, Old Silver Hump continued to swipe and rip at the hated remains of his tormentor. At last, groggy and uncertain, the grizzly left off punishing the muddy tangle of blood and sinew. He pulled back and reared up onto his hind legs once more, reaching to his full height. Then he dropped down onto all fours, turned weakly, and shambled off.

The great beast made it as far as the timbered ridge before he collapsed and died.

Colt in hand, Fargo dismounted and walked over to what was left of Red Ericson. The man's torso was still recognizably human, even though his left shoulder and arm had been completely severed from the rest of his body. His right hipbone, shiny white and flecked with red, stood out clearly.

Fargo had ridden back to finish the man off if this were needed. It was not. Fargo holstered his weapon. He had given Ericson a terrible death, but the man

168

had gone down fighting, and that was a better death than he deserved.

Fargo walked back to the pinto, swung into the saddle, and galloped away, leaving Ericson to the buzzards.

11

By the time Fargo rode through the high pass leading from the valley, it was snowing heavily. He wrapped a scarf around his face and kept an eye out for a campsite that might offer him protection from the wind. This time the snow-laden wind was howling out of the north with a far keener edge than it had possessed during the earlier storm. Screaming past him on an almost horizontal path, as soon as the snow struck the ground, it began to drift.

Topping a small ridge, Fargo became aware of a line of dim horsemen closing about him. Nez Percé. He pulled up and waited as the leader of the war party rode closer. Through his slitted eyes, Fargo studied the face of the warrior. He appeared to be a chief.

Fargo held up his hand in greeting. The chief paid no attention as he reached over and lifted Fargo's Sharps from his scabbard. Another brave came at

Fargo from his side and lifted his Colt. Cocking the revolver, the brave held the muzzle against Fargo's neck.

"Friend," Fargo told the chief, shouting so his voice could be heard above the storm. "I am friend to Nez Percé."

The chief leaned closer and studied Fargo's face. Then he waved the brave's gunhand down.

"You follow Indian," the chief told him. "We see if you friend."

With members of the war party on each side of him, the chief in the lead, Fargo rode on for at least an hour through the howling storm. His hands and feet were stinging from the cold by the time they dropped to a stream-watered flat close in under a peak. Not long after, Fargo saw the Nez Percé lodges materializing out of the storm.

A moment later, hands were pulling him from the saddle. He was dragged unceremoniously through the snow and hurled into a lodge. A small fire flickered in the center of it. Wasting no time, Fargo held his icy hands over it. Then he pulled off his boots and began to thaw his feet.

Fargo was almost warm when the flap was thrown aside and the chief entered, four of his warriors crowding in after him. Fargo got to his feet.

The chief came to a halt before him and studied his face. Behind the chief and despite the bitterly cold wind that whipped at them, curious squaws and children poked their heads into the lodge to watch.

The chief spoke first. "You settler?"

"No."

"You settler!" he insisted. "You bring in squaw! Soon, many children fill mountains."

"No."

The chief studied Fargo's face closely. "Nez Percé Indian want no settler in their land. Wagon go through. Blue coat go through. Settler stay. Build town. Sell whiskey to Indian. Take young squaw to sell in whiskey place. Settler no good."

"I am not a settler."

"Where is old White-beard? He ride with you, we see. Sometime he talk to grizzly. He have powerful medicine. But he not settler."

Fargo realized the chief was referring to Jed Two Shoes.

"He is dead," Fargo said.

The chief frowned and passed this information on to his braves. They appeared impressed by this knowledge. Then the chief looked back at Fargo. "You kill White-beard?"

"No."

"Who kill White-beard? Grizzly?"

Fargo had an inspiration. "The settler."

The chief nodded quickly. For the first time a grim smile lit his face. "I know settler you mean. He have crazy white woman for squaw?"

Fargo nodded.

"Settler bad. Kill friend of Tall Wolf. Settler and crazy white woman bring more settlers. Very bad."

"No," said Fargo. "The settler and the crazy white woman are dead."

This news was startling. It also appeared to please him. Again the chief studied Fargo's face. "Grizzly kill white settler?"

"Yes."

"Did not grizzly kill crazy woman, too?"

"No."

Tall Buffalo looked unhappily about him. "Is crazy white woman still up in valley?

"No. The settler killed her."

This admission sobered the chief. He told the others and they seemed equally impressed. To kill a woman who did not have all her senses was dangerous. Such people were deemed to have powerful medicine and were to be handled with great care, in some cases veneration. It was not good medicine to harm such people.

Tall Buffalo nodded sagely. "Settler kill crazy woman, grizzly kill settler. White woman have strong medicine."

Fargo saw at once what Tall Buffalo was implying: that the crazy woman's spirit returned in the guise of a grizzly and killed the man who had taken her life.

Fargo had no inclination to argue the point. Instead, he tried to put this interpretation to his advantage. "Now that settler and crazy woman are dead, I leave the high valley. I will not come again to this place. I am not a settler."

"Why you come to Nez Percé lands?"

"I search for two men."

"Why?"

"They killed my father and my mother. Many years ago."

The chief considered this. Then he appeared to sigh. "You search no more. Here you die with Nez Percé. Your spirit sleep. Like spirit of crazy woman sleep. And no more white man will know of high valley. It is good." He smiled then, his face creasing into a thousand wrinkles. "You will die like warrior."

Fargo thought of arguing with the chief. But he knew it was useless. The chief had it in his mind to do Fargo a kindness and at the same time save the valley.

The chief turned to leave the lodge. But as he did so, a young squaw stopped him and began talking rapidly in the Nez Percé tongue. The chief listened for a moment, then pulled the young woman into the lodge out of the howling wind and questioned her intently. Then other braves stepped close to her and continued the questioning.

The chief turned back to Fargo.

"What are you called?"

"Fargo. Skye Fargo."

"This squaw say you save her sister."

Fargo frowned. He did not understand.

"She say you save Flower That Is Wild from cruel white man. She say you kill all dirty men in whiskey place. So now all Nez Percé girls come back to their people. Many Nez Percé lodges are happy again."

It took only a minute for Fargo to realize that the chief was referring to the frightened Nez Percé bar girl with the pathetic wild flower stuck in her hair, the one who had been so brutally handled by Brad Poucher.

He nodded quickly. "I am glad the young girls come back. That was a bad place for them. Very bad."

The chief straightened. "Nez Percé drink no more whiskey. Sell no more girls. It is law with our people now. And you not die. You live!" He beamed. "You stay with Nez Percé until snow melt. Then you search for other bad white men. Tall Wolf has spoken!"

Once again, Fargo knew it would be useless for him to argue.

Wrapped in a warm blanket, his fire crackling, Fargo listened to the wind as it buffeted the tepee. Already, deep drifts had piled up all around the lodge, securing it more firmly as the raging storm prowled like some great demented beast through the encampment. This snow was here to stay, and so was Fargo—at least for a while.

Hell, he thought wearily. He could have done worse. Much worse. He could be out there lost in the midst of this blast, a frozen hunk of meat and clothing, bent over a futile hole in the snow where he had tried to keep a fire going.

As he drew the blanket more closely around him, the flap opened and a tall Nez Percé Indian woman wrapped in a buffalo robe stepped into the lodge. She regarded him for a moment, obviously pleased at what she saw. Then she turned and fastened the flap. Smiling down at him, she walked closer to him, opening the robe and letting it drop as she came. Then she kicked off her snow-laden moccasins.

She wore nothing under the robe. As slim as a sapling, her supple brown figure gleamed in the firelight. Her breasts were high, the nipples straining outward. She kept moving toward him. He sat up, nuzzled her dark, luxuriant muff, then reached up and pulled her down beside him.

Yes, sir. He sure as hell could have done a whole lot worse.

LOOKING FORWARD!
The following is the opening section
from the next novel in the exciting
***Trailsman* series from signet:**

The Trailsman #35
KIOWA KILL

1861—Some called it the corner where the
Utah and Wyoming territories touched.
Those who knew, called it Kiowa country and rode
the land in fear . . .

"Dammit to hell," the big, black-haired man bit out angrily as the pounding on the door continued. He swung his powerfully muscled naked form from the bed as Sally Dix pulled the towel up and her large, soft breasts disappeared. Or almost. It was a small towel, not really up to the task of covering Sally's ample mammary contours. "Who the hell is it?" Skye Fargo barked at the closed door of the hotel room.

"U.S. Army, sir," the voice called from the other side of the door.

Fargo's thick, black brows lowered in a frown. "U.S. Army?" he echoed.

"Yes, sir," the voice answered.

Fargo cast a frowning glance at the woman in the big brass bed, and Sally Dix shrugged bare shoulders at him.

He drew the big Colt .45 from the gun belt hanging over the brass bedpost. "Open the goddamn door," he rasped. He had the hammer pulled back as the door opened and the blue-uniformed figure stepped into the room. Fargo lowered the Colt as he took in the smooth-cheeked face, not more than nineteen years on it, he guessed. The soldier's eyes went to the bed, where Sally tried unsuccessfully for modesty under the towel. Fargo saw the young soldier pull his eyes away from her with an effort.

"Corporal Dexter, sir," the soldier said, standing stiffly. "Sorry to interrupt."

"That makes two of us," Fargo growled.

"Three," Sally said with a little laugh.

The corporal kept his eyes rigidly fixed on the big man's muscled form. "Captain Rogers wants to see you right away, sir," he said.

"Who's Captain Rogers?" Fargo frowned.

"Commanding officer, Troop B, U.S. Cavalry, sir," the corporal answered.

"Ten soldier boys, one barracks at the end of town," Fargo heard Sally put in.

"Well, Corporal, you tell the captain I'm busy," Fargo said as he returned the Colt to its holster. "And I expect to stay busy for some time."

"Begging your pardon, sir, but the captain said you should come right now," the corporal answered.

"The only place I'm going to come now is right

178

here, sonny," Fargo growled, and heard Sally's giggle.

He saw the corporal swallow. "But Captain Rogers said—" the soldier began again as Fargo cut him off.

"Pack it in," Fargo snapped. "You are putting off my pleasurin', soldier, and that irritates me. You've ten seconds to get out of here."

"Yes, sir," the corporal said as he bolted from the room with a last glance at the bed where Sally was already flinging the towel aside.

Fargo kicked the door shut and sank back onto the bed where Sally Dix's arms encircled his neck at once. "Damn, how'd that Captain Rogers know I was here?" he muttered.

"You brought in the Browder caravan. The whole town knows you're here, and there's but one hotel in Spineyleaf," Sally said.

"Suppose so," Fargo muttered as he lowered his face into Sally Dix's big, pillowy breasts. He rubbed his face into their enveloping softness, then pulled back, let his eyes travel up and down Sally's ample body. Always a large girl, Sally still had the body of a beautiful peach, everything round and delicate pink, luscious and soft. Only now it was a peach only a short time away from becoming overripe, the muscle tone in her breasts gone just enough to allow a hint of sagging, her legs a little heavier, belly a little rounder and fleshier. The years had been kind, but they still left their mark. Yet Sally Dix's direct, simple, honest enjoyment of the pleasures of the body remained the same as when she'd worked in a dance hall instead of owning one.

"Fargo, make the years all go away," she murmured as she pushed herself under him, lifted, and he felt the heavy, thick triangle press into him.

Her hands began to roam up and down his body, halting only to dig into his buttocks and push him toward her. Sally had never been one for slow preliminaries, he remembered well, and he moved into the soft avenue of her thighs. Her flesh closing around his waist was warm, and he felt his seeking organ pushing, probing, finding, sweet warmth, dark tenderness, and he heard Sally's groan of pleasure. He moved slowly with her, back and forth, caresses of the flesh, inner touchings. Her torso moved slowly with him, pushing down and upward, down and up as if in a slow, horizontal dance.

"Oh, yes . . . oh, yes . . . so good . . . so good . . . aaaah," Sally groaned, and Fargo saw her lips curl in a Cheshire-cat smile and remembered sounds came to him, deep little laughs, pleasure-filled sighs, as her hands continued to dig into him. "Ah, yes, ah . . . ah, good . . . ah, Fargo . . . Fargo, good, good . . . ah, yes," Sally Dix murmured with the happy little laughter, and he felt her movements take on quickness yet no frenzy, her torso pushing deeper, longer, as a giant wave takes on new strength when it nears shore. The warm pressure of her fleshy thighs grew stronger, pulled tight against him, and Sally Dix laughed, a roar of pure joy, another remembered sound. "Oh, Jesus, great, oh, great, wheee . . . oh, great," she half-screamed as she exploded with him—arms, legs, pillowed breasts all enveloping him—and he felt her head nodding vigorously in rhythm with her inner spasms of pleasure until finally she slowed, slid away from him, her hands moving along his ribs, legs rubbing slowly against him until they slipped away.

He pulled back and saw Sally's broad face smiling up at him.

"Just the way it always was, Fargo," she said, and sighed happily, pulled him against the large pillowed breasts with the firm, brownish nipples. "I thought I'd be rusty," she said. "Don't do it hardly anymore. I let the girls take care of that."

"Glad you made an exception in my case," Fargo said. She pushed her hands through his black hair as her eyes traveled over his chiseled handsomeness and grew suddenly almost sad. "You . . . you're old wine, Fargo. Can't ever turn down old wine," Sally Dix murmured.

"I'm holding you to your promise . . . a week," he said.

"It'll go too fast," she answered, kissed him, and pulled away to swing her legs over the side of the bed. She stood and reached for the lavender dress, pulled it on over her full bottom.

"What are you doing?" Fargo frowned.

"Got to go back to lock up the cash box. We put away the cash twice a night," Sally said.

"You never said anything about this. I figured you'd be staying the night," Fargo protested.

"For God's sake, I'll be back in an hour." Sally laughed as she buttoned up the dress. "You just wait there and think about it, and you'll be all ready to go when I get back."

"I don't have to think about it. I'm ready now," Fargo grumbled. "Hell, this isn't fair."

"I'll be back. You can wait an hour," she said as she pulled the door open and sailed from the room, still carrying her shoes in one hand.

He heard her little laugh as the door closed; he lay back on the bed and wiped the frown from his face as he thought about Sally. Six years since he'd seen her and suddenly it was as if it were only a few weeks back. The flesh makes its own remembering. But Sally had made her own life here in Spinyleaf, he reflected, a grub worm of a town with little past and an uncertain future. But then it couldn't be much more sitting in the middle of Kiowa country with the Wasatch Range behind it and the rolling prairie land in front. Bringing the Browder caravan out from Kansas had been an unexpectedly hard run, filled with flooding and detours, and traveling up through Medicine Bow to skirt the Colorado Rockies.

He'd earned his week of pleasuring, and he lay back and counted off minutes until the hour was almost gone. The hungers of the flesh and anticipation were a potent combination, and he felt himself responding as he lay naked on the bed and the hour drew to an end. The knock on the door was soft, feminine, and right on schedule.

"No need for you to knock, honey. I'm just waiting

for you," he called out. His eyes were on the door as it opened and she stepped into the room. He glimpsed a tan, high-buttoned blouse and very blue eyes turning into blue saucers, full red lips dropping open.

"Heavens!" he heard the young woman gasp as she stared at him, her very blue eyes focusing on his erect, almost waving maleness. "Oh, my God," she gasped as she spun and raced from the room.

"Damn!" Fargo bit out as he swung from the bed.

"Would you *please* put something on," he heard the voice call from outside the open door.

"Sorry," he said as he climbed into his shorts. "You just got the wrong room, honey," he said with a chuckle in his voice.

"You said you'd been waiting for me," the young woman called back.

"Expected some other gal," Fargo said, and stepped to the doorway. The young woman turned, her very blue eyes brilliant but full of disapproval as she stared at him.

"Can't you put trousers on?" She frowned.

"Not going anywhere I'll need them," Fargo said laconically as he let his glance take in a fairly tall, slender shape, breasts that pushed the high-buttoned tan blouse out in nicely rounded, twin mounds. He saw a thin, straight nose, delicate nostrils, light-brown, almost blond hair pulled up in a bun atop her head, pencil-thin brows that arched over the brilliant blue eyes, full, red lips that had no business being held as primly as they were—a strikingly attractive face despite the austere, severe, disapproving cast to it. She leveled a schoolteacher stare at him.

"Whether you were expecting some other young lady or not, no gentleman would invite anyone in in that state," she said.

"I'm not interested in any lecturing," Fargo said, his voice hardening.

"Those who need it most usually aren't," she sniffed with disdain.

"I told you, you just got your little high-toned ass in the wrong room," Fargo said.

"Obviously," she snapped as she started to turn away. "I was looking for Skye Fargo."

"What for?" he asked in surprise.

She paused, the blue eyes sheathed in icy condescension. "I hardly think that's any of your concern," she answered.

"Might be." He shrugged. "Seeing as how I'm Skye Fargo." He turned and sat down on the bed. He lifted one leg up, rested on his elbows. She appeared around the edge of the open door a moment later, the brilliant blue eyes staring at him, moving across his muscular, powerful body.

"You're not," she breathed.

"Sorry, but that's me," he said. "Now who in hell are you, honey?" he asked.

Her head lifted and she answered with a cold regality that might have done justice to a princess. "Millicent Madison," she said. "I left a message with the desk clerk telling you I'd be coming by this evening."

"Never got it," Fargo said, and chuckled as he recalled his words at her knock. "Few crossed signals," he said. "But you found me. Now you tell me why?"

He saw her eyes sweep over him with disapproval again. "I'm not used to talking to gentlemen clad only in their shorts," she said.

"Too bad," he commented, and saw the brilliant blue eyes flare. "Talk."

"I've a job for you, something that needs immediate attention," she said.

"You and the U.S. Army," he grunted, and she frowned.

"I beg your pardon?" she said.

"That translates into no," Fargo growled.

"You haven't even heard me out," Millicent Madison said.

"Don't have to. Not interested. Come back in a week," he said.

"I don't have a week to waste," Millicent snapped.

"Me neither." He grinned as he stretched out on the bed. "Go find somebody else."

"You can't just turn me down like this," she protested, the brilliant blue eyes darkening.

"I just did, honey," he said.

"What do you have to do here for a week that's so important?" Millicent demanded.

"Screw, sleep, and eat, in that order," Fargo answered.

"You enjoy being crude?" she snapped.

"I enjoy being honest." He smiled.

"A life is at stake here," Millicent Madison said.

"Nothing new about that out here, honey," Fargo said.

"And you won't even hear me out?" she accused.

"I told you, come back in a week," Fargo said. "I've earned my pleasuring. I'm going to enjoy it."

"I can't wait a week and you're a callous lout," Millicent half-shouted. She pulled the door open wider and stalked out of the room. "You're something, Fargo, really something," he heard her call back, and a half-second later he saw Sally's face appear, instant fury gathering in her eyes as she glanced back down the hall and then at him as he lay in his shorts across the bed.

"You bastard," Sally Dix hissed.

"Now, hold on, there," Fargo said as he swung from the bed, Millicent's heels still clicking down the hallway. "You've got it all wrong."

Sally's eyes held fury and he remembered the wildness of her temper. "You couldn't even wait an hour. You had to go get some chippie from the hotel," she said. "All that bullshit about waiting so long to see me again, and I believed it."

"She just came to offer me a job," Fargo said.

"Offer you something, but it wasn't a job. I heard what she just said. You're something, Fargo, really something," Sally mimicked.

"She didn't mean what you're thinking. You've got

it all wrong, dammit," he tried again, and saw the rage stay in Sally's eyes.

"You sure haven't changed any, I'll say that, except maybe for the worse," Sally blazed. "Your week just came to an end, you bastard."

"No, wait, listen to me. You've got it all wrong. Look, I'll go find her tomorrow. I'll get her to tell you herself," Fargo said.

"Meanwhile, you'll try to screw and sweet-talk me into forgetting and forgiving. You go to hell," Sally flung back. "You bring her to me tomorrow, let me hear her say it, and then we'll see. Till then, don't you come nosing around my place, you hear me?"

"Come on, wait," he tried, and reached for her arm. She pulled away from him and stalked into the hallway. "Goddamn, this ain't fair," he yelled.

"Hah! You're someone to talk about fair," she threw back as she strode away. She reached the stairway and he started to race after her and halted, realized he was only in shorts. He turned back into the room to yank on trousers, gun belt, and boots. Seconds later he was racing down the hallway to take the stairs in three leaping strides. The lobby door was still swinging as he raced outside.

"Dammit, Sally, you hold that powder-keg temper of yours," he shouted as he ran into the street. He skidded to a halt as the six uniformed figures blocked his way, each holding an army carbine. He saw the young, smooth-cheeked corporal at the end of the line.

"Captain Rogers' orders, sir," the corporal said.

"He told us you weren't to leave the hotel except to go with us."

Fargo's eyes went over the six soldiers, none much older than the corporal, he saw, all young faces distinctly uneasy. He cursed under his breath. He didn't want a shootout with the army, not without a hell of a lot better reason than this. "I just want to catch that gal that ran out of here," he said.

"Sorry, sir," the corporal said.

Fargo's eyes were narrowed as he slowly scanned the line of troopers and came back to rest at the corporal. "Corporal Dexter, you know who you're playing games with?" he asked.

"Yes, sir, we've been told about you," the soldier said, and Fargo saw him swallow hard.

"Then you know I could take out at least four of you, maybe more, with my first volley," he said.

The corporal swallowed again. "Yes, sir," he said.

"And you're going to try and stop me," Fargo commented.

"Captain's orders, sir," the soldier answered. Fargo's grunt gave him credit for fighting down the fear that was so clear in his young face.

"You've more guts than brains, sonny," he muttered. "Then I won't be leaving till morning."

"Whatever you say, sir," the soldier answered, but the relief was plain in his voice.

"Goddamn," Fargo muttered as he turned and strode back into the hotel, almost tearing the door from its hinges as he slammed through it. The room shook when he reached it and slammed the door shut. There was a back stairway, but that still left Sally to argue with and he knew there'd be no convincing her this night. He turned the lamp out, flung clothes off, and lay down on the bed to curse Sally and her damn temper. But Millicent Madison had been the blame for it, he bit out in silent anger. Her damn unexpected visit and her parting words. Signals crossed all over the place, he thought, frowning.

He swore again and turned on his side, closed his eyes, and let sleep slowly creep over him. It was the only thing the night held for him, now. But come morning, he'd find himself a high-nosed, lecturing little prude. She'd help him put his week back together or he'd have her ass for it.

JOIN THE *TRAILSMAN* READERS' PANEL

Help us bring you more of the books you like by filling out this survey and mailing it in today.

1. Book Title: _____

   Book #: _____

2. Using the scale below, how would you rate this book on the following features? Please write in one rating from 0-10 for each feature in the spaces provided.

POOR		NOT SO GOOD			O.K.			GOOD		EXCEL- LENT
0	1	2	3	4	5	6	7	8	9	10

                                                                RATING

Overall opinion of book .... _____
Plot/Story .... _____
Setting/Location .... _____
Writing Style .... _____
Character Development .... _____
Conclusion/Ending .... _____
Scene on Front Cover .... _____

3. About how many western books do you buy for yourself each month? _____

4. How would you classify yourself as a reader of westerns?
   I am a ( ) light ( ) medium ( ) heavy reader.

5. What is your education?
   ( ) High School (or less) ( ) 4 yrs. college
   ( ) 2 yrs. college   ( ) Post Graduate

6. Age _____   7. Sex: ( ) Male ( ) Female

Please Print Name_____

Address_____

City _____ State _____ Zip _____

Phone # ( )_____

Thank you. Please send to New American Library, Research Dept., 1633 Broadway, New York, NY 10019.

Exciting Westerns by Jon Sharpe from SIGNET

(0451)

- ☐ THE TRAILSMAN #1: SEVEN WAGONS WEST   (127293—$2.50)*
- ☐ THE TRAILSMAN #2: THE HANGING TRAIL   (110536—$2.25)
- ☐ THE TRAILSMAN #3: MOUNTAIN MAN KILL   (121007—$2.50)*
- ☐ THE TRAILSMAN #4: THE SUNDOWN SEARCHERS   (122003—$2.50)*
- ☐ THE TRAILSMAN #5: THE RIVER RAIDERS   (127188—$2.50)*
- ☐ THE TRAILSMAN #6: DAKOTA WILD   (119886—$2.50)*
- ☐ THE TRAILSMAN #7: WOLF COUNTRY   (123697—$2.50)
- ☐ THE TRAILSMAN #8: SIX-GUN DRIVE   (121724—$2.50)*
- ☐ THE TRAILSMAN #9: DEAD MAN'S SADDLE   (126629—$2.50)*
- ☐ THE TRAILSMAN #10: SLAVE HUNTER   (114655—$2.25)
- ☐ THE TRAILSMAN #11: MONTANA MAIDEN   (116321—$2.25)
- ☐ THE TRAILSMAN #12: CONDOR PASS   (118375—$2.50)*
- ☐ THE TRAILSMAN #13: BLOOD CHASE   (119274—$2.50)*
- ☐ THE TRAILSMAN #14: ARROWHEAD TERRITORY   (120809—$2.50)*
- ☐ THE TRAILSMAN #15: THE STALKING HORSE   (121430—$2.50)*
- ☐ THE TRAILSMAN #16: SAVAGE SHOWDOWN   (122496—$2.50)*
- ☐ THE TRAILSMAN #17: RIDE THE WILD SHADOW   (122801—$2.50)*
- ☐ THE TRAILSMAN #18: CRY THE CHEYENNE   (123433—$2.50)*

*Price is $2.95 in Canada

Buy them at your local

bookstore or use coupon

on next page for ordering.

Wild Westerns by Warren T. Longtree